LIES
OF THE
BLOOD
MOON

NEW WORLD SHIFTERS
BOOK TWO

NINA WALKER

KIMBERLY LOTH

LIES OF THE BLOOD MOON

NEW WORLD SHIFTERS BOOK TWO

KIMBERLY LOTH

NINA WALKER

PROLOGUE

I'VE ALWAYS BEEN A RISK-TAKER. As a kid, I swam where I shouldn't swim, climbed where I shouldn't climb, and asked too many questions—until the day my parents sat me down and explained the importance of weighing my risks before taking them. They said I was old enough to understand that I needed to stop being reckless. I didn't like the lecture, but when my mother left the room to get supper started, my father said something that I've never forgotten. He kneeled down, looked me square in the eye, and said that one day risks would outweigh staying safe, and when that happened, I needed to be brave.

Today is that day.

And so was yesterday, and the day before, and every day since I was claimed by the Carolina Pack. I will *not* go down without a fight.

"There is no way in hell that Nova's death was an accident. None," I whisper angrily, my voice carrying over the water more than I'd like.

"But it's not possible they found out," Lexi whispers back as she scrambles into the boat behind me.

We go quiet as we untie it from the dock and let it drift out into the black water for a few minutes. Once I'm sure it's safe, I start the engine. I keep thinking about her response but don't bother to answer because it's totally possible the wolves found out about Nova. Not only possible, it's *probable*. Nova fell in love with one of them—not that I can really talk. I fell in love with Grady, but he has no idea the danger I put myself in every day. And I'll never tell him.

Maybe Nova told Nico.

Then again, maybe it really was an accident, or she killed herself like they want everyone to believe. I shake my head at the thought, and the night breeze bites at my cheeks.

The boat hums along softly as we head into town. I always worry about getting caught, but since we're going toward the city and not away from it, we're less likely to look suspicious. Lexi and I can both say we are sneaking out to visit the betas, but then we'll have to explain how we know how to operate a boat. We could say we learned it in our villages, but that argument is flimsy considering I'm from the textile village, and she was a farmer. And of course Madame Delphine would have to punish us, but we wouldn't be killed. That's the main thing.

And anyway, her punishment would only be for show since she's one of us.

I guide the boat to a dock near a nice house on the outskirts of town. We tug our hoods up and hurry for the house. We usually do this close to the new moon, when there's hardly any light, and it's unlikely we'll be seen. Tonight, however, the moon is a few days from when it was full. I resent that it lights up the landscape. Maybe it doesn't matter either way. Light or no light, it won't help us if one of the wolves roaming the outskirts sees us. Monsters can see in the dark.

The floral scent hits me as we approach the house. Shauna loves her flowers. My mother would be so jealous of her long-lost sister. Mom never could get anything to bloom so early in the season.

We skirt around the house and head for the greenhouse in the back. Each member's arrival time is staggered so no one will become suspicious. We don't want any neighbors to take notice. Lexi and I are always the last to arrive, which is nice because that means we don't have to wait for the meetings to start, but I wish I had more time to spend with Shauna. She reminds me of home.

A large man looms next to the greenhouse. He's so still that he could almost be mistaken for a tree in the darkness. He's a wolf. And he's the only one who knows about us. At least, I think he's the only one who knows. Sure, plenty of wolves know *of* us, and many are trying to hunt us down, but Shauna's husband is the only one we can trust. I'm still pretty low in the ranks of the Resistance, but I've been assured there aren't other wolves involved. That's good, because how can we really trust them?

I even wonder about Grady sometimes...

And then I feel guilty because he's proven himself more devoted to me than I ever thought possible. I have no doubt that he's madly in love with me. But what would he do if he knew the truth? Would he still feel the same? Still protect me? Or would his loyalties lie with the pack?

Our resistance group has about twenty women, and there are other groups that meet all over the city, in other wolf cities, and even out in the wilds. That's all I know about our numbers—we have to be careful. It wouldn't be safe for the other groups to know too much about us or vice versa. All it takes is one weak link, and the whole chain breaks to pieces.

But Nova was one of us, so we can't delay this. We need to come up with a plan.

"Hey, kids," Amos whispers as we approach. He ruffles Lexi's hair but knows better than to do that to me, even though I'm his niece. We shake hands. "You doing okay?"

Lexi and I nod.

And all things considered, we are. I've got Grady, and Lexi is consistently on top of the scoreboard. She's the smartest of the claimed girls, so she aces every class.

"Any word from the other cities?" I ask. I always ask even though the answer stays the same. I think we should band together and revolt.

"Go on inside and find out for yourself." He chuckles, avoiding my question yet again. "You know how she is about things. I keep my mouth shut and stand guard, and that's it."

I roll my eyes. He's talking about Shauna. Apparently there's some secret way she communicates with the other leaders so that we all have the same information, but she doesn't share how many women are involved or all the little details. My parents are a part of the Resistance. When I was claimed, they wanted me to go willingly and stay safe until they could think of something. Yeah, right. I'd fought those bastards on day one, but I ended up with Grady, so I guess Mom and Dad got their wish.

Or not... because I found the Resistance as soon as I got here.

We enter the greenhouse and find the trapdoor in the back. It's been propped open, and a ladder sticks out the top. I eye it wearily. It's not far down, but I still get a little claustrophobic descending the rungs. I sigh and climb down quickly, and my feet hit hard earth.

I duck into the cramped stone tunnel and then out

into a large room lit with lanterns. This hiding place is quite brilliant, but Amos and Shauna can't claim it as their idea. It belongs to the brave humans from hundreds of years ago, those good people who smuggled slaves to safety.

The room is nearly full. Several women are crying while others are consoling them. I should be among the women crying––Nova was my friend––but anger forced the tears away.

Someone murdered her. I know it.

Shauna's head snaps up when she hears us. "Oh good, you're here." She hurries over and hugs me, kissing me once on the cheek. It's weird having her in my life suddenly, but also comforting. She was taken by the claiming before I was born, so to find her here was a small miracle in all of this. She steps away and gives me one of her winning smiles. She's a pretty middle-aged woman and looks so much like my mom sometimes it hurts.

"Ladies, we need to get started." She walks to the head of the crowd, her head low for a moment, but then raises it. A few tears glisten on her cheeks. "Two nights ago, we lost one of our own. It's not the first time a woman in the Resistance has been murdered, and it will likely not be the last."

"We should find and kill the bastard who did this to her," I call out.

Shauna glowers at me. "That's not our way, and you know it."

I cross my arms and frown. The Resistance has always moved slower than I would like. They focus on rescuing women and getting them away from the wolves, but it's not like they can do very much of that. I think we should be attacking. In fact, we should burn the whole city to the ground.

But no one listens to me.

I keep my mouth shut as Shauna continues. "Delphine, you knew her best. Do you think we've been compromised?"

Madame Delphine steps from the shadows. She knows Lexi and I come here, but she always travels on her own by town car. I wish she wouldn't. I'd feel safer if we all came together, but she says this is better. And she'll *never* talk about anything back at the manor, so it's not like I have much time to convince her otherwise. "No. I knew Nova, and there is no way she told anyone, including Nico."

And I would agree if it weren't for all the times I've wanted to tell Grady. I understand how hard it is to keep something like this from a fated mate. But then again, I saw Nico's reaction when Nova's body was pulled from the river. He was completely shocked.

And he was heartbroken. Can't fake that.

Shauna purses her lips and nods. "Okay, then onto business. Who needs rescuing this week?"

"Everyone," I snort quietly to myself. Then I tune out as they talk. They never let Lexi or me assist with any of the rescue missions. Madame Delphine always puts a stop to it when I volunteer. I'm so sick of doing nothing. Even back in the textile village, I had more of a role than this nonsense.

After a while, the conversation dies, and I see my opening.

"I have a new recruit."

Madame Delphine raises her eyebrows but doesn't say anything.

"Who?" Shauna asks.

"My friend Poppy."

A few of the women look at me from the sides of their eyes. Everyone knows who Poppy is because of the stunt Ryne pulled on the Wolf Moon. Gossip travels fast even in the mating houses.

"Haven't you tried to get her out of the city a couple of times?"

I clench my fists. Those failures were not my fault. "Yes. She's decided she wants to join us instead."

"Absolutely not," Madame Delphine cuts in.

"Why not?" I protest. Poppy is ready for this. She has motive and is an incredible fighter. If you ask me, we should be recruiting more heavily than we are. The more we have, the better chance we'll have to fight them.

"Because she's too young. You and Lexi shouldn't be a part of this either. I will not allow another one of my girls to join. If, after the Harvest Moon Festival, she still feels the same way, then she can join."

"After the harvest, she might be in the mating house, if not earlier. If she's part of the Resistance, then she'll have an easier time escaping if she needs to—before she's been raped by a hundred wolves."

A few women flinch, but no one says anything. We should use that word more freely, if you ask me. Why not call it what it is?

"I will see to it that she doesn't end up in a mating house, but she cannot join us." Madame Delphine presses her lips tight.

"She's ready. We need—"

"Joanna," Shauna snaps. "We saw what happened at the wolf moon. The alpha either has a special interest in her, or he's saving her for his number two, but either way, Poppy isn't someone we can bring into our fold. What would happen if she were caught by one of them? She could lead them right to us, even unwittingly."

"But—"

"That's enough." Her voice is understanding but stern.

I don't argue because it's pointless, but this isn't over.

Poppy will become one of us.

CHAPTER 1

POPPY

UNLIKE SO MANY other humans who've been lost to this bleak city, Nova actually gets a funeral. I stand along with the other girls, bracing against the cold, on the edge of Nico's family plot. We're a line of modest black, our heads down, as Nico drops a handful of clumpy dirt into Nova's grave. The late January sky is a blanket of white, and the air smells of ice and salt. The wind bites through our wool coats, and it seems unfair that the cold would come out and be so distracting on Nova's day. Most of the girls are crying, but my tears seemed to have frozen with the winter. A few words are said. A prayer is offered. And then it's time to go.

We're ushered to Anders's home for refreshments. His estate is at the edge of town, and it's especially grand, almost as grand as Ryne's, but I don't care. This last week following Madame Nova's death has been the most somber of them all. That is two house mothers who have died since coming here, not to mention the girls we've lost. It's such a tragic accident, though whispers suggest it could've been something more. Classes were canceled all week, and we barely saw Madame Delphine until today.

The betas—and Ryne—never came to see us. Joanna hasn't said anything more to me about the resistance movement, and I haven't asked. Grief has overtaken us all. I stand in the corner of Anders's living room, hoping to be invisible while peering through the window out toward the horizon. Nova shouldn't have died. What possessed her to go out to the river, anyway? Maybe she just needed time to think. Or maybe she was meeting with a member of the Resistance. Some say she killed herself, but I don't think so. And others say she was murdered.

Whatever happened, Nico deserved better, and so did she.

People mingle in small circles, whispering in hushed voices. Wolves come and go, offering Nico their condolences. Some of the wolves flirt with the girls, but I stay back. I won't be caught flirting at a funeral. And I can't help but wonder if anyone will notify Nova's family back in her village.

Probably not.

She's been gone from them for so long anyway;

they've likely mourned her already. I wonder if my family has mourned me.

Ryne is there, but he doesn't look at me. I avoid him anyway. Everytime I think of him, I think of that kiss and how desperately I want another one. And then I feel guilty because I should be thinking of Nova, not him.

Sometime later, we're loaded up and brought back to Drayton Hall. It may be the first time I'm grateful to be taken here. All I want to do is crawl into bed and go back to sleep. Nova's death has reignited the feelings of loss and guilt I have about Willow. I don't think I've uttered a single word all day, and I don't want to. What is there to say? It's a tragedy. I'm going to miss my friend, I desperately miss my sister, and everything is unfair. We eat dinner, and they send us to the sitting room to keep each other company. I just want to be alone.

It's late Sunday evening, and tomorrow we start classes again. As much as I hate what's happened, I'm relieved to get back to some semblance of normalcy. Joanna and I sit in the corner and read. This time, I'm able to get most of the words. Even though I'm slow, reading is a nice distraction from the pain and thoughts of Ryne. The other girls spend their time gossiping. Joy, one of the distillery girls, mutters something about Nova that catches my ear, especially when everyone else in the room goes quiet and stares at her. No one had uttered Nova's name in here since she died.

"What?" Joy furrows her dark eyebrows and glances around at all the stares.

"What did you say about Nova?" Joanna asks since no one else does. She's not being accusatory, just curious.

"What no one else will. Now that she's gone, Nico will choose one of us. It's a blessing really."

I jump up, but Joanna jerks me back down. She has no right to think those things right now. Nova's barely in the ground.

Joy sniffs. "What? Not all of us have bewitched the alpha's best friend and can count on a kiss to save us from the mating house. We need all the chances we can get."

A few of the other girls nod in agreement.

Katelyn clears her throat, and everyone looks at her. I don't think I've ever heard her say a word. She's now at the bottom of the board. Well, just above me. "But if Nico was so bad that Nova had to kill herself to get away from him, do we really want him?"

"Nova didn't kill herself. She loved Nico," I snap.

"How do you know?" Faye asks, with her arms crossed.

"Because she told me."

"If she didn't kill herself, you know what that means, right?"

"What?"

"She was murdered." Faye smirks like it's obvious.

"Nova accidentally falling into the river makes no sense."

"Who would murder her?" I ask, but I'm not sure I want the answer.

Faye scoffs. "Duh. Who had the most motive? It had to be one of us."

Every single one of us had a motive to kill Nova, but are any of the girls that ruthless? Maybe, if they know what is coming. I shiver at the thought of what Ivy and Callista must be going through right now in the mating house. That should've been me. But I would never kill someone.

We all look at each other, uncomfortable and suspicious. I take a deep breath, the scent of polish and perfume and fear filling me up. This is bad. Really bad. If some of these girls start thinking their best way to get a beta is to kill someone, then it'll turn into a bloodbath. I squeeze Joanna's hand, and she squeezes right back. Footsteps pound up the stairs, and Madame Delphine enters the room in a flourish. We all stare at her, and none of us says a word about murder, though I'm sure we're all thinking it. Joanna is the only one in the room who had no motive to kill Nova.

"Ladies, classes resume tomorrow. Your new instructor will arrive late this evening, and I hope you will show her the same courtesy you showed Madame Nova. She's the daughter of an old friend of mine from the Chicago Pack. Also, the betas will be by in the morning as well. They'll be spending more time here. Now that the first cut has happened, and you've all had some training, they want the opportunity to get to know you individually, not just on group dates. I will be creating a schedule so you all get time with each beta."

I don't want to spend any time alone with Anders. Truthfully, Ryne is the only one I want to be around. And I know how wrong that is—he's the Alpha. He's forcing us to be baby-makers against our will. It's all evil, and he should've stopped it a long time ago. And I should hate him, but try telling that to my heart. That kiss was everything.

"What about Grady?" Faye asks, and Joanna stiffens next to me. I know she's in love with him, even if she pretends she's not.

"Well, as we saw with Madame Nova, nothing is guaranteed, so he will be on the rotation." She waves her hand in a circle.

My stomach sinks. I didn't think about what Nova's murder would mean for Joanna. If one of the girls did kill her, then Joanna could be next. I squeeze her hand again, but this time she doesn't squeeze back. Her lips are set in a thin line, and her eyes narrow on Faye. My best friend is mad as hell.

"It's time for bed. You've had far too long of a break, so be ready to run at six tomorrow."

A collective groan goes out among the girls, but I like to run.

Joanna and I escape to our room, and as soon as the door clicks shut, I pounce on her. "You have to be careful."

She strips off her shirt and digs in a drawer for pajamas. "Why? If you ask me, Faye is the one who should be careful. I seriously hate that girl."

"I mean it, Joanna. Whoever killed Nova might come after you next. It's got to be a girl who understands what happens in the mating houses and wants to make sure she doesn't go. And for all we know, that could be Faye."

Joanna slips a nightgown over her head. "That's ridiculous. These girls don't have the nerve."

"You're telling me that you think Madame Nova killed herself?"

"No way. But none of the girls here killed her. It was one of the wolves." My heart stills. I suppose it's possible, but I think Faye had a better idea. Not that I'd ever tell her that.

"Why would they kill her?"

"Because they are all assholes."

"I don't think so. They had no reason to. But the girls here all did. If she was killed because she took one of our betas, then that girl will have reason to kill you as well. And if she managed to kill Nova, then she's got skill."

Joanna sits on her bed and leans forward. "Listen, I know you're worried about me, but you shouldn't be.

You should be worried about the girls who are going to spend one-on-one time with Grady."

"Why?"

"Because if one so much as bats an eyelash at him, I'm going to kick her ass. I don't need points, so I don't care if I end up at the bottom."

I want to laugh at her snarkiness, but I can't. She's not seeing the real danger here. But Grady will. I have to tell him.

I really hope that Joanna won't hate me for doing so.

"I'm serious, Joanna. I think one of the girls did it." And we need to figure out who before she kills someone else. Like Joanna.

She snorts. "Think about it. Nova went outside alone on a night when all the wolves were out. One of them probably killed her simply because they saw the opportunity and took it."

I look down at my hands. I'm not sure the pack's telepathic link works like that. If a wolf killed her, he'd have to be really good at keeping his secrets. Maybe I should ask Ryne about all this. I sit down on my bed. "Either way, don't you think she deserves to have her murderer outed?"

Joanna stills. "What are you saying?"

"We should investigate."

She folds a shirt, avoiding my eyes for a moment. "Okay. But we have differing opinions on who did it, so why don't you take the girls, and I'll see if I can find out any information on the wolves."

I think she's wrong, but at least she's on board. Even if she won't investigate the girls with me, I'll be able to talk things through with her at night.

I let out a breath.

Never in a million imaginations did I ever think I'd be hunting a killer.

<hr>

My shoes pound the dirt running path as I push my body to move faster. My muscles scream from the exertion, and my face burns from the cold. It's bitter out and early enough that the sun hasn't fully risen. The black sky lifts away with each step I take, the horizon slowly transforming to pink. I know the running path well enough that I don't worry about tripping, so I forge ahead until I've left all the other girls in my wake. I don't mind being alone. I don't want to talk to any of them, and Joanna refused to get out of bed this morning.

She insisted she started her period and is having terrible cramps, but I wonder if that's true. Every time Joanna strays from the group, I'm going to assume it's got something to do with the Resistance. I'm a little hurt that she hasn't talked to me about the organization more, but I trust that she will when the time is right. She knows I want in. That hasn't changed in spite of my feelings for Ryne.

How large is the Resistance movement? Do they have any chance against the wolves? It might be so small that nothing will happen for a very long time, but I don't care. I want to take down the wolves. They've ruined my life and countless others. And I don't care if I die in the process.

Maybe it's because of Nova's death, but Madame Delphine didn't make Joanna get out of bed. I worried a little bit about leaving her alone because it would be the perfect opportunity for whoever killed Nova to attack her, but she insisted I leave. I have to talk to Grady before it's too late. He'll be better at protecting her than I am.

Not that he should have to. This whole pack dynamic is wrong, and nobody should be forced to fight for a beta or spend their days in a mating house. This has to change. *It has to.*

All I can hope is that in the process of revolution, Ryne makes it out alive. I can't undo my feelings for him, as much as my mind knows he's hurt me and others. I still think—still know—that there's a part of him that wants things to change as much as I do. Is he a bad guy? Or is he forced to be bad, but he wants to be good?

It's all so confusing.

I push myself to go even faster, because it forces the thoughts away. It's hard, but I love it. I love the cold air, the rushing blood, and the pumping muscles. And I even love running alone, but that quickly changes when a streak of silver darts right in front of me and out across the grass. I stop abruptly, my heartbeat pounding against my eardrums. What was that? I peer into the field, but there's nothing there.

Did I imagine it?

I shake my head and begin running again, this time even faster. I feel like something is chasing me. That's silly though. There's nothing there.

But what if there is?

My mind races, thinking about the lycans, but it's not the full moon. A wolf then? Are wolves silver? I've seen quite a few over the last three months, and they're always black or brown or sometimes dark gray. This was definitely silver, as bright as the moon. I shiver at Joanna's word that it was a wolf that killed Nova, not another girl. What if that wolf is after me?

But that's silly because I have about as much chance at scoring a Beta as Madame Vivien does. And she's probably sixty already.

Another flash passes through the field, this time black. I don't think it sees me, but I definitely see it well enough to know it's a wolf. The wolves all look similar to each other, but I swear that's Ryne's wolf. He's heading in the same direction that the silver went, up over a hill and into the forest. I should turn back and find the other girls, but curiosity gets the better of me, and I race after them.

I creep into the trees and listen intently, pushing away feelings of foolishness and worry. I want to see what Ryne's doing here more than I care about any of those feelings. I'm pretty sure that silver flash was a wolf. Are they fighting? Is Ryne in trouble? That thought gives me speed, and I race through the trees. The sound of a wolf excitedly barking stops me. I peer around a tree and find them in a clearing.

Ryne's big black wolf circles a smaller silver one. His blue eyes stare into the other's amber ones. They bark and then pounce. At first I think they're fighting, but then I realize they're playing. The smaller wolf pins Ryne down and howls. It steps off him, and they stand on all fours one second, and then with a flash of light and fur, they're shifting into their human forms--completely naked. I shouldn't look, but I can't stop myself because I'm surprised by what I see.

The wolf is a woman.

CHAPTER 2

"ELLE MONTGOMERY," Ryne laughs. "I knew that was you." He pulls her into a hug, still naked as the day he was born, and the two laugh. His eyes shine with excitement and what I think could be love when he looks at her. And why not? She might be the most beautiful woman I've ever seen. She's petite and curvy all at once. She's got smooth ebony skin that seems to glow gold in the sunrise. Her long black hair is braided down her back, and her sparkling eyes are the exact color of my mama's homemade caramel.

She's a wolf. I can't seem to wrap my head around that. I thought all wolves were men. I can't stop staring at her. Her presence changes everything. If women can be wolves, then what do they need us for?

"It's good to see you too, Ryne. Look at you, all grown up." Even her voice is perfect.

I can't stay here. Jealousy claws at my heart and shreds my stomach. The two start talking animatedly, and I back away slowly until I can safely turn away without getting caught. I meet up with the running path again, and the other girls are just catching up.

Faye rolls her eyes when she sees me. "Did you have to pee?" The others laugh and pass me. Joy blows me a kiss. I guess she's Faye's new sidekick now that Ivy is gone.

I don't try to pass them. I do a slow jog. My mind is a mess of questions, but the biggest is this: What is Elle Montgomery doing here?

The mystery of Elle distracts me from what I really should be thinking about—who killed Nova—but I can't help myself.

Wolves are never female. That's why they have to take the claimed in the first place, to keep their race from dying off. My mind races through the lessons we've had about wolves, and I stumble when the truth hits me. One out of a hundred wolves is born female. We've never met one, but that doesn't mean they're not out there. And this one seems to know Ryne quite well.

I hit the showers and try to think of anything but Ryne and Elle. I'm unsuccessful. The image of the two hugging while naked is burned into my brain. I have no claim on Ryne, but after the kiss we shared, I feel like I do, and I don't want another woman anywhere near him. I walk back into our room wrapped in a towel, and

Joanna grins at me. She holds up two dresses. "What do you think, the black or the black?"

They are exactly the same. I force a smile. "The black definitely."

She doesn't seem to notice that I'm not all there. So much for her having cramps and not being able to get out of bed. We dress, and I stick close to Joanna as we head down to breakfast. I haven't forgotten there is possibly a murderer among us, and that Joanna could be the next victim. I have to keep an eye on her until Grady can. He'll protect her. But first, I have to warn him.

If I can pinpoint the murderer, it will be easier to protect Joanna. Katelyn is the most obvious suspect since she is near the bottom of the board, but really it could be anyone, because this isn't about those who get sent to the mating houses at the festivals. This is about who gets a mate come the harvest.

Hopefully we'll have combat again soon, and I can keep an eye on girls who do well. They'd have been more likely to overpower Nova than a girl who can't even punch someone in the gut.

Madame Delphine walks into the room with Elle Montgomery. She's managed to find clothes. Somehow, she even looks good in the black wool dresses we often wear on the days the betas aren't coming around. Has she come to join us in our training? If a female wolf is getting added to our crew, she's bound to get a beta. I grimace, wondering what that means for the rest of us.

"Ladies, I want you to meet Madame Elle. She will be your new house mother." Madame Delphine beams at her.

Elle gives us a wide toothy smile and a small wave. I release a breath, grateful I'm not going to have to compete against this beauty. She looks to be no older than any of us, but her energy is worldly and mature. I find it strange that they would bring in another barren woman after Nova's death. Is she barren? I have no way to know. I thought all the house mothers were, but there's something different about Elle, that's for sure.

Aside from the obvious wolf thing.

"Like I said last night, she's the daughter of a dear friend of mine, and I want you all to welcome her to our little family."

I snort. Some family. We keep getting killed.

"What you don't know about Elle is that she's a luna. That means she's one of the rare female wolves. She's here to offer extra protection and will be living among us."

The girls are especially excited by that and start to applaud Elle, who responds with a little curtsy. I can't help but roll my eyes at the way the others suck up to her. Joanna and I sit down at breakfast in our usual spots, and Elle finds a place right across from us, where Nova used to sit. I want to tell her to go away, that that seat should always remain empty in honor of Nova, but she's our fancy new house mother, so I don't.

"Did you come from a mating house or what?" Joanna shovels a big bite of biscuits and gravy into her mouth. I want to say something about Elle being a wolf, which means she's probably treated like a princess. All I can think of is what I saw between her and Ryne this morning. It replays in my mind in a loop. I fork my meal with a little too much ferocity.

Elle's ever-present smile falters. "I've never stepped foot in a mating house. Why would you think that?"

Joanna chews and swallows. "Because I thought the house mothers were either barren or done having children. You're young, and I don't see a ring on your finger. I assumed you were like our old house mother, Nova. She came from the mating houses. Right, Poppy?" Joanna nudges me.

"Right."

Elle drops her eyes and swallows. "Oh, no, I hope I'm not barren. I've never been to a mating house or with a man for that matter, so I wouldn't know."

Joanna nods. "Yeah, I thought all fertile women were to be out there making babies for whoever wants them. No offense, but you've got to be prime real estate to these men."

She sits up tall. "I'm a luna, and I make my own choices."

"Lunas can make their own choices?" Joanna asks, disbelief lacing her tone. Not for the first time am I grateful that Joanna is my friend. She asks all the questions that I wish I could. That girl is fearless.

"Uh, duh. She's a female wolf," Katelyn says from the other side of Elle. "She's special enough to get to do whatever she wants."

Elle looks away at that, and I wonder how much Katelyn's statement is actually true. Either way, I'd argue we're all special and should be able to make our own choices. I keep the thought to myself.

Joanna's lips curl into a wicked grin. "That's pretty amazing. Welcome to our dysfunctional family where you and the other house mothers prepare us for a life of whoring."

Half of us laugh, and half of us stare at Joanna like she's lost her mind. Elle frowns.

"My mother and father thought it would be good for me to get out of the city for a little bit," she confesses with a sigh. "I think they were tired of the parade of men who came to our door every day. Quite frankly, I was a little tired of it as well." She plays with her food before meeting Joanna's eye. "Tell me about the girls. You seem to be very knowledgeable about the goings-on in this house."

I nearly roll my eyes—again. Joanna will love this woman. Being a know-it-all and being recognized for it? It's her only flaw.

Elle seems very nice, and I want to like her, but my stomach burns every time I look at her. I saw the way

Ryne looked at her, like her arrival was the best thing to happen to him in ages. And they were naked!

My jealous musings are interrupted by Joanna. She's good for that.

"Well, let's recount, shall we? There were twenty-two of us to start, but two got kidnapped by lycans on our very first day. A month later, one of our girls turned into a lycan herself, killing two more girls, one of our house mothers, and biting a third girl who had to be put down." She uses air quotes for that last part, giving a little scowl. "She got away in the end. Then we lost two more girls to the mating houses at the last festival, not to mention that our beloved new house mother, Nova, turned up dead in the river." Joanna bats her eyelashes. "So, Elle, are you sure you want to be here?"

Elle gapes at Joanna and motions to all of us sitting at the tables. "I'm already aware of the deaths. I meant the girls who are still here. I'm supposed to help protect you guys."

Joanna winks. "Oh, I know. I just thought you should be aware of what you're getting yourself into." She takes a deep breath. "Okay, so at the end of the table, closest to the door, you have Faye, Joy, Blair, and Emma. They are the distillery girls, meaning they came from that village and think they're better than all of us. They sit over there because they want to be able to spring on the betas when they arrive. Next to them are the wannabe distillery girls, Raven, Alyssa, and Abi.

Then there's Lexi and Samantha. Those two are the teachers' pet types. They couldn't care less about the actual betas. They only want to be top of the leaderboards to prove they're the smartest. My bet is they end up taking each other down before this is all over."

Joanna pauses for a moment to scan for any girls she missed. "Oh,"— she points to a back corner of the room —"and that one with her nose stuck in a book is Bailey. She's really nice, but she's super shy with the guys and really good at tuning the rest of us out with all that reading." And she's right. Bailey leans over a novel as she eats her breakfast, her eyes glued to the book. The girl is completely unaware that we're even talking about her.

"Then you'll notice several empty seats in the middle of the room. No one sits there because we don't want to be near each other. Down here, you have me and Poppy. I'm Grady's fated mate or whatever, so I can do whatever I want. Poppy is my best friend and at the bottom of that disgusting board, so if you wanna hang with us, you have to promise to help her."

Elle's smile grows even wider. "I'll remember that. I like you, Joanna, so I will do what I can to help Poppy. But you missed these two lovely ladies." She points to the other side of her to the two girls who always sit on this side of the room near us, as well.

"Oh, that's Katelyn and Harlow. They're wannabe rebels like me and Poppy."

"Hey, that's not true," Katelyn says. "We just don't

want to be like them." She nods to all the girls sitting by the door and gossiping among themselves.

Elle nods. "Fair enough. So we have the distillery girls, the wannabes, the teachers' pets, the book girl, and of course, the rebels." She tilts her head at me and smiles brightly. "Tell me, Poppy, what are your best subjects?"

I'm having a hard time warming up to this woman because of Ryne, but she *is* trying. "Anything physical besides yoga. Combat is my favorite."

"Yeah," Joanna adds, "Poppy is our resident athlete. She keeps us all on our toes."

"Well then, I will mention to Ryne that you girls need some more serious combat training. That should help you move up the board."

Katelyn groans because she stinks at combat, but we ignore her. I don't know how I feel about Elle talking to Ryne about anything, least of all about me.

"How do you know Ryne?" Joanna asks. I'm grateful to her once again for peppering Elle with the questions I can't bring myself to ask.

She giggles, and her eyes sparkle with memories. "He used to visit my family when we were kids. He teased me horribly. I see him every time he visits Chicago, though he hasn't been there in years. But we talk on the phone all the time. He's probably the closest thing I have to a best friend. There aren't many girls my age, and all the men I know want to marry me." If she had mentioned a phone to me a few months ago, I wouldn't have the foggiest what she meant. But Madame Delphine has a phone she uses all the time, so I've since been schooled on the technology.

"Does Ryne want to marry you?" Joanna asks. She plays it off nonchalantly, but Katelyn, Harlow, and I wait for her answer.

Elle scowls. "I don't know how Ryne feels, but our fathers certainly want us to marry. Mine's been planning on it for years. It might be the one thing I won't get a choice on, and if I didn't like Ryne so much, I'd probably hate him."

Her words tunnel in on me, and I set my fork down, no longer hungry. I don't care how nice Elle is, and I don't care that she's a beautiful luna—*Ryne is mine*. I shake my head, trying to clear the possessive thought away, but it clings to me like static. I'm not sure where it came from, but I still can't shake the feeling that Ryne and I are fated mates. That would explain the insane jealousy I'm feeling. I know I should be thinking about Nova and who killed her, worried about the leaderboard, planning my next step with the betas, but in this moment all I can think of is that kiss and how badly I want to punch Elle in the nose for even entertaining the thought that she could be with Ryne.

And I have to know the truth about Ryne and me.

The need to take action is so strong that I can no longer sit here and listen to another woman speak Ryne's name, especially not one who's known him since childhood, who makes him laugh and smile, who's been *naked* with him, and who will probably marry him. The chair screeches as I get up to take my plate to the kitchen. I'm shocked by my own feelings.

"What's her problem?" Emma questions mockingly as I pass by them.

"She's obviously jealous. Poor girl thought Ryne liked her and I know all about Elle. She's Ryne's fated." Faye's voice follows me as I push my way into the kitchen. I clean my plate and give it to the staff and then head out the back door. There are still a few minutes before we're due to class, and I need to think.

Better yet, I need to find Ryne.

CHAPTER 3

IT'S cold without my coat. The bitter air bites every inch of my exposed skin. I almost turn back, but then I catch some wolves racing through the nearby field, and I run after them.

"Ryne!" I yell at the big black one with the glacial eyes. "I need to talk to you right now!"

A couple of the other wolves bark and grow quiet. It's as if some kind of communication is passing between the alpha and his betas, because they look at him for a long moment and then scamper off all at the same time. Ryne changes into his human form. I should turn away while he grabs some shorts from a nearby pile of clothing. I've always been shy in the past, but this time I don't. He belongs to me, anyway. I know it.

Funny how it took jealousy over Elle to realize it.

He grabs my arm and drags me away from listening ears. "You can't summon me like that. It makes me look weak. Besides, we can't talk about this right now, Poppy."

"You've been avoiding me ever since our kiss."

His expression turns stony. "You're going on a date today with Justin. And then you'll be dating the others."

"But—"

"But nothing," he growls. "I saved you, and you should show an ounce of gratitude for that."

But *he* kissed *me,* and it wasn't for Anders like he told everyone. I've been going over it again and again in my head. I think he used Anders's infatuation with me as an excuse to save me, for his sake, not for Anders. When we were at his house that night, he caught Joanna and me trying to run away, but he didn't punish us. No, he held me and told me he would be kissing me when the time was right. Saving me from the mating house certainly wasn't because of his betas.

He wants me as much as I want him, so why is he denying us?

"I don't know what to say," my voice cracks.

"Don't make this harder than it has to be."

My heart squeezes, but I'm not the same timid girl I was back in September. Something has changed within me over the last few months, and I'm no longer going to let others stop me from taking what I need. I may not be able to find the right words, but I can use actions to show him how I feel. I step forward, grab his face, and bring his lips to mine.

The weight of him crashes over me in a wave of relief. His lips are quick to move against mine, to claim me as his. He growls and deepens our kiss. See? This is exactly what I've been talking about. I know he feels it too. This feeling isn't normal. It's not just an infatuated kiss. It's fate. But all too quickly, he rips away and takes several steps back.

"When are you going to understand, Poppy? My betas are the best I can offer you." His voice thickens. "I can't keep saving you. You need to step up and do your part to save yourself. Now get inside before you catch your death."

Then he turns away and shifts back into his wolf, his clothes ripping to shreds in the process. I guess he cares more about getting away from me than he does for his belongings.

He runs off after his betas, and I storm back into the house. All the while, I press my fingers to my lips and try to memorize the kiss. If I could tattoo the feel of him to my lips, I would. Ryne says the best he can do is offer me a beta. I know it must have something to do with Elle and his father, with being an alpha, with everything that's expected of him and that he expects for himself. Well, a beta for my husband is not going to be good enough for me. Maybe in the past, but not anymore. Living with anyone other than my mate would be a false life, and I'm not going to settle for less than the real thing.

I don't care what it takes. I'm going to get Ryne to admit the truth, and then I'm going to make him do something about it.

I find Bailey reading in the library. It's as good a time as any to get started on my investigation, even if I am still mad as hell at Ryne. Anyway, I doubt Bailey's the killer, but I'm not ruling anyone out. She's a good person to start with because she won't get upset with me for asking questions. And I need to do something else besides obsess about Ryne right now, or I'll lose my mind.

I go over my plan in my head again. I'm telling the girls that I'm collecting stories about Nova to share with Nico. This would be more believable if I could write, but the villagers have been telling stories for years orally, so it's not that far-fetched. Last night I asked Joanna for help interviewing the girls, but she flat out refused and reminded me that our plan was for me to talk to the girls and that she was handling the wolves.

I squeeze my hands into fists and then stretch my fingers out. I don't know why I'm so nervous. Maybe it's because a part of me is afraid I'm going to find the killer and that she'll know that I know. And then what? Will she come after me?

I sit in the chair next to Bailey. She doesn't look up from her book. Lucky little thing learned to read in her village but never had access to as many books as we do now. She's probably worked her way through half the library. She reads like she's running out of time. Maybe she is.

"Hey, Bailey," I say gently.

She tears her eyes away from the page. "Yeah?"

I watch her carefully. "Listen, I'm collecting nice stories about Nova to share with Nico. Do you have any?"

It's a good alibi. At least, I hope so.

At first she just looks at me with a blank stare. Then a single tear rolls down her cheek. "She was always so nice to me, recommending books to read and talking to me. Almost everyone else ignores me. Even the teachers, but she didn't."

I nod, believing every word. That sounds like Nova.

"What was her favorite book?" I ask. I can already tell there is no way Bailey killed Nova, so that's one girl off the list. Well, three because it wasn't me or Joanna either.

"*Emma* by Jane Austen," she says and drops her eyes again. I don't know that book, but I make a mental note to read it as soon as I'm able.

I place a hand over hers. "She was my friend too."

She sniffs. "This is really nice of you to do for Nico."

I nod and stand. Time to hunt down the other girls.

Even if I don't find out another single thing about who might've killed her, I'll have stories to share with Nico.

———

Katelyn and Harlow were also easy to cross off my list. They both had good stories about Nova and cried when telling them. I suppose they could be acting, but it's the initial reactions that I'm looking for, and I'm not finding any reason to suspect them. They also don't seem like the murderous type.

It's hard to get Faye and the other distillery girls alone, so I approach them as a group. They are sitting at a table in the dining room, painting each other's nails. The stench in the room is a little overwhelming.

I sit next to Blair, and she glares at me. "I'm not painting your nails, so shove off."

"I don't want my nails painted. I have a question."

Faye scoffs. "We probably don't have the answer."

My initial inclination is to look down, but I have to watch their reactions.

I look Faye right in the eyes. "I'm collecting nice stories for Nico about Nova and was wondering if you had any."

Faye doesn't react. Joy drops her eyes, and Emma fidgets with a bottle of paint, but no one acts suspiciously.

Then Faye laughs out loud. "I knew you were a

sneaky one." She leans back and crosses her arms. "You killed her, and now you're going to use your friendship with her to get in good with Nico. You know, if you were my friend, I'd be impressed, but you're not, so get out of here." Shame burns in my stomach even though she's wrong about the motive. Because I see how it might be taken and I don't want everyone else thinking the same thing.

"Are you kidding? I'd never kill Nova. I'd never kill anyone."

Faye glares. "I said get out of here, and I meant it."

I want to argue, but I'm never going to get anything out of them. I should know that by now, but her accusation still stings. I shove my chair back and storm out of the room. I'm getting nowhere. I head out the back door because I need some air.

Lexi is painting at an easel in the middle of the grassy lawn. She's got quite the talent for it and has been painting every spare moment she can get. I watch her for a minute, finally deciding that just because those girls made me mad doesn't mean I can quit. The killer is likely one of the distillery girls, so right now all I have to do is rule everyone else out. Even if they think I'm doing this just to get to Nico.

I jog across the field and approach Lexi. She jerks her head up when she sees me. "What do you want?" she asks. She sounds more defensive than unhappy to see me. Maybe she can sense what I'm here for.

I can't see what she's painting because she's facing me, and the easel is between us. She's always been a little grumpy though, so the tone of her question doesn't catch me off guard. I don't move any closer.

"I just wanted to ask you if you knew any nice stories about Nova."

"Why would I know anything about her," she snaps.

"I'm asking everyone," I say.

Her whole body tenses.

"For Nico," I continue. "I want stories about her for Nico."

"Well, I don't have any," she says with more force than necessary.

"Are you sure? She was your teacher too."

"No. I don't know anything, and I have no idea why you think I would."

I think back to the scoreboard. She's always been fairly high up on the board because she's good at lessons, but she's never seemed to catch any of the beta's attention—except Nico. I'd forgotten about it until now, but before Nova arrived, he always sat next to Lexi. She's a smart girl, and they seemed to get along well, talking about the kind of stuff that goes way over my head. But it doesn't matter how smart you are. The scores on the board mean nothing if one of the betas doesn't choose you in the end. We all know that. Lexi knows that.

"Okay, well, if you think of anything, let me know," I say brightly. Then I turn and walk away. I don't run, even though I want to. I act like everything is normal, like I have no idea what Lexi has done.

Because I'm pretty sure I've found Nova's killer.

CHAPTER 4

THE BOAT ROCKS, and I grip the edges, trying not to get sick. But the rowboat is tiny, and the waves are rough. At least they seem that way to me. Justin whips his fishing pole back and flings the tiny fish on a hook into the water. The movement reminds me of going fishing with my dad. Inevitably, Willow would jump into the water, and Dad always said that she scared the fish away. The memories flood me, and I force myself to refocus on Justin before my eyes fill up, and he wonders what's wrong with me.

This isn't exactly my type of romantic date, but then again, I'm not looking for anything romantic with him, even though I should be. He's said hardly anything to me, and we've been on the water for thirty minutes now. I have a cloak wrapped around myself, but it's still cold on the water.

"Do you fish often?" I ask.

"When I have time, which, no, isn't often. The older claimed women do a lot of our cooking for us, so there is no need for me to come out and catch my own, but I do enjoy it. I figured we'd catch a few and then cook them over a fire on the beach."

So maybe that is slightly more romantic. But still. Any conversation that includes the claimed doing his cooking for him isn't attractive. The longer I'm here, the more I see this evil for what it really is. But I need to stay focused, so I continue the conversation.

"How did you learn to fish if you grew up here?"

"Oh, my mom is from one of the fishing villages. She taught me when I was a child, and we still go out sometimes."

"You still keep in touch with her?"

"Of course. We all do. You know Ryne sees his mom all the time." It's not a secret anymore that Madame Delphine is the alpha's mother.

I didn't realize that if I had a child with a beta, I'd still get to see him as an adult. That makes me want it even more. But at this point, I'd only want it with Ryne.

"I wish I could see my mom again," I mutter. And my dad and little Evan. I wonder how much has changed since I've left. Maybe everything. Maybe nothing.

He sticks his fishing pole into a slot and plops down next to me, rocking the boat way too much for comfort.

He slides his arm around me and tugs me close. "I know. I wish you could too, but that's simply not the way it's done."

The line of his fishing pole suddenly goes taut, and he hops up. He wrestles with the pole a little bit, and a large shiny green fish pops out of the water, thrashing.

"Grab the bucket," he yells.

I glance around, find the bucket, and hold it out. He drops the fish, and its tail flicks me. I jump and nearly drop the bucket. Justin laughs. "It's only a mahi-mahi. It won't hurt you, but it tastes amazing."

I peek into the bucket and grimace. It doesn't look very tasty. "I'll take your word for it." I adamantly refused to eat fish growing up, which drove my parents mad. Luckily, Willow ate enough for both of us.

He laughs again. This is the happiest I've ever seen Justin. I can't help but smile.

"No. You'll love it, I promise. We'll go back to my mom and dad's house, and I'll have her cook it. I won't do so hot cooking it on a fire out on a beach, and you deserve to taste mahi-mahi as it was meant to be."

"Your parents are still together?"

His face softens, laugh lines bunching around his pale green eyes. His blonde hair shines under the sunlight, and I suddenly realize how attractive this man actually is.

"Yeah. They are fated mates. No way Dad would ditch her now."

"Won't it be weird, taking me to meet them?"

"Why would it be? You're potentially my wife. It makes sense that I would introduce them to the girl I like."

I swallow. This escalated fast. "Wife? I thought you were going after Faye."

He raises an eyebrow. "She's definitely still a contender, but there's still a long way until the harvest moon. Ryne saved you. That must mean you've got something special. And I didn't realize it before, but you do. You're much easier to be around than Faye, and I doubt she'd be willing to hold the bucket while I fished."

We both laugh at that.

Faye's a challenge, and I have a suspicion that's exactly what Justin likes about her. And maybe that's why he's suddenly developed an interest in me—because now I'm a shiny prize to be won too. I'd much rather be won by him than Anders, but my heart tells me that's wrong. I belong to Ryne.

Justin catches two more fish, so we finish up and head out to his parents' place. A driver takes us across town, and we sit in the backseat and talk on the way. The fish are in a cooler in the trunk, but I can smell them anyway. I hate that smell, and after the seasickness from the little rowboat, my stomach isn't liking the idea of dinner. Hopefully his mom is good at preparing them to mask the taste. Considering we live near the coast, I probably can't avoid fish my whole life. Maybe eighteen years is all I'm going to get.

Justin and I don't have a lot in common, so the conversation is a little forced. He's used to girls fawning over him, so he goes for the ones who don't make it easy. I don't know how to do either of those things. All I can manage to be is myself, and maybe he finds that boring because at one point, he yawns.

"Do you have any brothers and sisters?" I ask, hoping to liven things up. One thing I've learned is that these guys love it when the conversation is focused on them. I expect this question to perk Justin right up, but his face goes ashen.

"Why? Has anyone said anything?"

"Uhh—no," I falter. "I'm just curious."

He relaxes and leans back in his seat. "Sorry. I didn't mean to get so defensive about my little brother."

"I understand. I'm defensive about mine too."

"Oh?" He frowns as if he's not put much thought into the fact that the girls who come here have families back home. But maybe I'm being too hard on him.

"Yeah, he's a cute kid. I miss him." And I do. He was always running around after me and Willow. A weight settles in my stomach.

He looks out the window, his mind somewhere else. This is about him, not me.

"Can I ask why you got defensive?" Okay, that was inappropriate. I hold up my hands. "Sorry, you don't have to answer that. Sometimes my curiosity gets the best of me."

"No, it's okay. I can't expect you to know everything about pack culture." He thinks through his words for a moment before speaking. "The thing is, there can only be so many betas at any given time. We can't have too many because we need a lot more deltas and gammas. So it's only the first-born son of a beta wolf who can get a beta spot, and that's only if there's availability. More often than not, those boys still have to fight it out. And as for second borns, well, they're always sent to the gamma barracks when they come of age."

"So I take it your little brother is a gamma."

Justin stares at his hands. "He was for three years, but he was killed last year when he tried to fight for a position as a beta."

My stomach turns, and my vision is filled with memories of the battle arena and all those bodies piled up. It's all so senseless, especially for an organization that claims it's doing everything it can to grow its numbers. And each of those dead? They might not all have families, but they all have someone who cares about them. And if they don't, well, that's a damn shame.

"Most betas have a lot of kids, but my parents only had two, and Dad refused to take another mate." He frowns. "So now it's just me."

"I'm really sorry, Justin." Even though our lives are wildly different, this is something I feel in my soul. I lost my sister and he lost his brother. There's a connection there that wasn't before.

He shakes his head and smiles. "Let's not talk about this anymore. We're here to have fun, remember?"

"Right." And Justin is a fun-loving kind of guy. He doesn't want a date who brings up the grief in his life. If I'm going to land a beta, I'd better learn to have fun.

I can't forget what the betas want. They want pretty. They want refined. And they want talented, strong, and subservient. Sometimes I worry that I'll never be those things, and now that Justin is taking me to his parents' place, that worry surfaces. Surely, his mother is perfect if she landed a beta. Will she judge me? My heart begins to speed as the realization hits me. If I don't impress his parents, I'll lose this chance with Justin for good.

CHAPTER 5

WE ARRIVE AT THE HOUSE, and I can't help but grin, my fears slightly dissolving. "It's really pretty."

His smile quirks as we get out of the car. "Thanks. I'll tell my mom you said that. This place is her pride and joy."

"Oh, you're not her pride and joy?" I tease.

He laughs and leads me to the front door. I stop right before we get there, leaning down to sniff a bright yellow rose. I didn't even know roses could look like this in winter. They're not always easy to grow. It offers a rare moment of magic in an otherwise drab world. I stand, and Justin smirks at me.

"What?" I ask.

He leans over and whispers in my ear, "Mom's watching from the window, and you just sniffed her roses."

"Was I not supposed to?"

But before he can answer, the door flings open, and the largest man I've ever seen ducks under the frame and steps out. He's all bulky muscle and towers over us like a mountain. "Son, another one? Your mother isn't going to be happy."

But his face splits into a grin, and he embraces Justin. He lets go and eyes me. "Just kidding. I'm Amos. Welcome to my home. What's your name?"

"Poppy." My voice cracks.

"Isn't that a flower?"

I nod, and Justin flinches. I have no idea what's going on. A tiny woman shoves past Amos and Justin and peers up at me. She's pretty with bright blonde hair and a friendly face. She must've gotten pregnant with Justin when she was first married because she doesn't look a day over forty. And maybe that means Justin isn't as old as some of the other betas. I never thought to ask. Or maybe this woman looks young because she's lived a life of luxury, and I'm used to being around women who labor.

"I'm Shauna. Did I hear you say your name is Poppy?" she asks excitedly. Her eyes dance a bit, and they remind me of her son's.

"Yes."

She grabs my hand and pulls me away from the house and into the yard.

"See you in a few hours," Justin calls with a laugh.

I'm still thoroughly confused, but his mom doesn't let go of my hand as we wind through bushes and flower beds out to a greenhouse. She drops my hand as we go inside and brings a small plant over to me with a bright red flower. She hands it to me. "For you. A poppy."

My chest warms. I've never even seen the flower I was named for. "Thank you. I didn't know what they looked like."

"Well, now you do. Do you like flowers?"

"I do, though I don't know much about them."

"I saw you admiring my Julia Child."

"I thought that was a rose."

She scoffs. "There are hundreds of different kinds of roses. I've managed to grow forty-three. Every night Amos and I come out and cover them up so they don't freeze. It keeps them blooming all year long."

"Wow. Will you show them to me?"

Her eyes light up. "That would take all day, and I assume Justin expects me to cook for everyone. But next time, for sure. If I give you a book about roses, will you study it? Then maybe you can tell me what they are when you come back."

"Of course." The idea of being quizzed makes me a little nervous, but I'm glad she seems to like me.

I don't know why, but I want to impress this woman. I don't tell her I can't read very well, but I'll have Joanna help me. Then again, Shauna's been in my shoes. I wonder what fishing village she's from.

We walk slowly back to the house and onto a deck with a sliding door that opens right into the large kitchen with deep black countertops and shiny appliances. I think back to my own mother cooking over a fire. This world still shocks me sometimes.

Justin and his dad are standing at the counter, dropping the fish into some kind of batter. "Stop," his mom shrieks.

She rushes forward to take over, but Amos catches her.

"Let me through," she demands. "You're going to ruin it."

He leans down and gives her a long kiss. It's a little uncomfortable to watch, but at the same time, I can't draw my eyes away.

Justin groans. "You get used to it. Seriously, do you have to gross her out?"

They break away, and his mom giggles while she brushes her hair out of her face. "It's been thirty years, and I'm still not used to it."

My insides sour. I want that. I want to be with Ryne, whose kisses I'll never get used to. Instead, I'm here with Justin, who is turning out to be a good guy, but I doubt he'd ever make me feel like that. And quite honestly, I think he wants it as bad as I do. He's a ladies' man with us, but seeing him here with his parents makes me wonder if that's a cover for something more genuine. And now I really hope he doesn't end up with Faye. If I were in his shoes, seeing my parents as fated mates, I'd probably wait until I found mine. Justin is young, so it's not like he has to take a mate yet. I wonder why he chose now to do so.

"I want to teach you something," Shauna says. She shoos the boys away and begins to rummage through her cupboards. "I know I have some somewhere." She pulls out a little jar of black seeds and grins triumphantly. "Poppy seeds!"

I can't help but mirror her smile. The black seeds are so small, and it's hard to imagine that something so stunning can come from something so small and seemingly insignificant. "What are those for?"

She finds a few more ingredients and shows me how to make her favorite salad dressing. We mix it in with the fresh greens from the greenhouse garden right on time for the fish to be finished. And then she does something unexpected. She hands me the jar with the seeds.

"These are for you. I know there is a greenhouse out at Drayton Hall. Find an old pot and plant them. You can move them outside in a few weeks. And then when they start to wilt, harvest the seeds for yourself."

I can feel my lips tugging at my ears, my smile so big. "Thank you. That's such a kind gesture." I set the little jar down on the counter for later. "Do you grow all your own food? I thought that's what we used the villages for?"

"Most of it. That's why I had Amos build me the

greenhouse. So that I could have fresh vegetables year-round." She pinches her lips in thought. "Honestly, I don't like to add any strife to the villages. I know how hard those people work. I was one of them, same as you."

Nobody really talks about the villages and everything we had to give up when we left home as the claimed. I can't help but ask, "Do you miss it?"

She sighs. "Yes and no. I miss my family. The people. I don't miss the hardship or the cold winter nights without much to keep me warm. And I can't imagine my life without Amos or my children." She shakes her head. "Did Justin tell you about his little brother, Jonathan?"

"Yes. I'm really sorry."

She wipes a tear. "Me too." The room has gone quiet. Something thuds outside, and she peers out the window. The men are out chopping wood. "Good, I'd hoped we'd get a chance to be alone after I got to know you a little better."

I stare at her, and she turns to me with a knowing gaze. "Your friend Joanna is my niece," she says, catching me completely off guard. I don't know what to say. Her cheeks pink, and she rushes on. "My little sister got married to Joanna's father and moved to the textile village around the same time I was brought here as one of the claimed. I didn't even know my niece existed for a long time. I had no contact with anyone back home for years. It was lonely." Her eyes shine.

"Don't mistake me. I love my family here very much, but there's always been a separate hole for the ones I lost to the claiming."

I smile sadly. "Yes, I know what you mean. I think we all do. Have you seen her?"

Her smile falters, and she drops her eyes. "No, I haven't," she says a little too quickly. There's something in her tone that doesn't quite match her words.

"I'm sorry."

She shrugs. "That's the way of things. What does she look like?"

I step back. "Well, for starters, her hair is short." Shauna doesn't look up at me. That surprises me because most people are shocked by Joanna's short hair. We are supposed to leave it long. "She cut it off and said she would rather die than become claimed, but her fated mate saved her life. The short hair actually suits her, although they're making her grow it out. Joanna is pretty and feisty and my best friend since coming here, not to mention she's the best-dressed girl in our house. Sometimes she—"

"Please don't say anything to anyone," Shauna cuts me off. "I can't let people know that I found out about her. They'd have questions, and I don't want to bring my family into things that could come back to hurt them later." She twists her hands together and goes back to the food, plating it carefully so that it looks perfect on the bright white china. "Did you know it's quite difficult for a beta to lie to his alpha? Some say it's impossible, but that's not true."

"So does Justin know?"

She shakes her head. I want to ask about Amos, but I expect the answer is the same.

She studies me for a long moment, as if deciding how much she can trust me. I don't know how much I can trust her either. I want to ask if she's with the Resistance, but I don't dare take the risk. If she's not, it could be disastrous. But somehow, I think maybe she is.

"Of course I'll keep it a secret," I whisper.

We take the plates to the table right as the men step back into the house. "Wow, Mom, it smells amazing in here," Justin says, and when he grins at me, his father waggles his eyebrows, and his mother winks. The two men must have been talking about me out there. What did they say? Whatever it was, I'm sure it couldn't have been as dangerous as the words Shauna and I exchanged tonight.

We eat the amazing dinner, one that doesn't even taste like the fish I've had before, and then Justin drives me home. He walks me to the doorstep and leaves me with a whisper-soft kiss. His lips are cold. I kiss him back because it's what I'm supposed to do. It doesn't seem to matter. My mind is elsewhere. All I can think about is the Resistance.

Is Shauna one of them? Does Justin know?

The wolves can take us from our villages and strip us

of our dignity, they can divide us and pit us against each other, but at the end of the day, we're still village girls in our hearts. If a beta's wife living in a grand house is missing her family enough to break the rules and risk her life, how many other women in this city would be willing to fight to obliterate those rules completely?

CHAPTER 6

IT'S a sunny Tuesday afternoon when I finally find the time to go out to the run-down greenhouse. It's smaller than Shauna's and hasn't been touched in years, but I instantly love it. I vow to fix it up and get it running again during my free time. The walls are dirty, the plants are dead, and the watering system is probably busted. It's going to be a lot of work.

I'm one million percent up for the challenge.

I start by washing out a few pots and filling them with rich, dark soil. The earthy smells and thick humidity remind me of home, and I feel like a kid again. My mind fills with memories of the fields that stretched out around my village, of those magical blue-skied springs when we'd plant the seeds for the new year. It was hard work, but I loved having a role to play and getting to do it alongside my family. The best part was watching a tiny seed turn into something people needed. Maybe sometimes that's how change happens; maybe everything starts out small and seemingly insignificant and turns into something worthwhile.

And maybe that's why the Resistance will eventually succeed.

But there's nothing I can do about the resistance until Joanna lets me. For now, I should focus on what I can do.

Take care of Nova's murderer.

I wonder how I can get Lexi to confess.

Joanna pops her head in the door. I told her about my suspicions last night, and she thought I was jumping to conclusions. I think I have pretty solid evidence, but she just doesn't want it to be one of the girls because that puts her in danger. I also have to find a way to warn Grady about this.

She's dressed in a cute white tennis skirt and leans against one of the tables with a long sigh, a racket in her hand. "We've been looking all over for you."

"We?" I ask.

Grady and Justin tromp in next, also dressed in athletic gear.

"Yeah, we wanted to play a game of tennis and need a fourth."

"Sure." Tennis is one of the games we've learned since arriving here, and I'm pretty good at it. There's a court in the field out back, and it's become one of the most popular activities for the girls during free time as the weather has started to warm. I like it too, but right now my mind is set on my task.

Justin comes over and wraps his arms around me from behind, resting his chin on my shoulder. I tense at his sudden affection. It doesn't feel wrong exactly, but it doesn't feel right either. "You're planting the seeds Mom gave you?"

I nod and try to think of how I can gracefully get away from him. Then again, maybe I don't want to. The more time I can spend with him, the less time I'll have to spend with Anders.

Joanna scoots closer. "How long will they take to grow?"

I'd told her all about our date, but I left out the part about learning she's Shauna's niece. I have to be careful about what I tell her. Joanna has a mouth and a short temper, and I don't want to break my promise to Shauna. The last thing I'd want to do would be to get someone in trouble. But part of me wonders if these two women already know about each other. If my suspicions are correct and they're both Resistance, then it stands to reason that they do.

"As long as I take care of them, they should start sprouting in a week or two," I say, hoping it's true. I'd love to see those bright red poppies here. I'll plant them along the wood's edge for future claimed girls to enjoy.

Joanna pops up on the table next to me and peers

down into the pot. "Well, hurry up with all this. I want to get my blood flowing."

Grady stands next to her and nuzzles her neck. "I can think of a few things we can do to get your blood flowing."

She giggles and swats him away. Then she jumps down off of the table. "We're going to go get started. Come join us as soon as you're done."

"Okay." As soon as they leave the greenhouse, Justin lets go of me and takes Joanna's vacant spot. He seems more serious today. It's not something I've seen on him before.

"Mom wants me to bring you back to the house."

I smile. "I barely saw them, what... A week ago?"

"I know. But they like you." He scoots closer to me and brushes a stray piece of hair away from my face. "I like you."

I don't want to put him off. He's exactly who I should be going for and someone who can save me from a life at the mating house or with Anders. But his touch isn't Ryne's. I hate that I have to fake it with him, but I do. And I need to do it well.

I lean into his touch and move a little closer to him. "I like you too," I whisper. He visibly relaxes and tugs me away from the pots I'm working on. I stand between his legs, and he brings me close. I wrap my arms around his back and close my eyes.

When his lips meet mine, I try to lose myself in the

kiss. I really do. It's nice, but it doesn't have the fire that I feel with Ryne. I wonder if I can grow to love Justin. Probably. I wonder if I'll ever stop comparing him to Ryne. Probably not. But I have to. Ryne has made that clear. My life depends on me moving on with another beta and letting Ryne move on with Elle. Because I've finally accepted that Elle's the reason why Ryne doesn't want me.

Justin breaks away and smiles sheepishly before jumping off the table and grabbing my hand. "It's time to go kick Grady's ass at tennis."

"We're playing Joanna too."

"I've watched you. You're good at anything athletic. Joanna doesn't stand a chance. She'll probably stand back and let Grady do all the work."

"Don't let her hear you say that." I giggle and lean into him because that's what I'm supposed to do.

We exit the greenhouse, and I spot Faye and a few of her friends playing croquet with Anders and Nico. She sees us, and I swear her face turns several shades of red. As if I don't need another reason for Faye to despise me, now I've got her favorite beta holding onto my hand like it means something. I drop my eyes and cling tighter to Justin.

———

"Keep your grimy paws off my man," Joanna says,

brushing out my hair. She'd bounded back into the room a few minutes before and snatched my brush out of my hands. It's the weekend, and we have dates again tonight, but I hadn't known who I was going out with.

I guess I do now.

"Don't worry. Grady knows I'd kill him if I ever caught him so much as looking at another girl that isn't you."

"That's my girl." Joanna winks at me in the mirror.

All things considered, it's been a pretty decent week. Elle made good on her promise, and we had combat twice more than normal. Add that to the points Justin gave me on our date last week, and I am now middle of the board. This is a step in the right direction, but my heart still lurches every time Ryne enters the room.

Which he does nearly every day now. He's with Elle a lot, but I feel his eyes on me all the time. And I can't help but look at him. It's like we're magnets, but we're forced apart because of their unofficial betrothal. But what hurts the most is that Ryne hasn't tried to call it off with Elle. So I guess I have my answer.

At least nobody else has died since Nova. At least, not yet. I still worry about Joanna.

"What do you know about tonight?" I ask her, but I already know the answer.

"Only that you're going out with Grady. I made him promise to give you a good score, but seriously, keep your hands off of him."

It's a joke, of course, but she doesn't have anything to worry about. I'm glad I'm going out with him because then I can warn him about Joanna's safety. I hadn't had any time to do that yet. This would be the perfect time for us to discuss it.

I wink back at her. "Who knows, maybe by the end of the night, he'll forget that you're his fated mate and take me as his wife instead."

She swats me on the arm. "That's not funny."

"Ow. I'm just joking. Better me out there with him than Faye."

Faye had actually been on a date with Grady earlier in the week, and Joanna and I spied on them when they came home. Faye tried to kiss him, but he turned his head, and she got his cheek instead. I had to lock Joanna in our room for the night to keep her from trying to fight with Faye. I'm pretty sure Faye knew we were watching, and that's the only reason why she did it. Everyone knows Grady's taken, but Faye loves to push Joanna's buttons.

"I swear. I should punch that girl," Joanna says, "or better yet, let's shave her head while she's sleeping. You know she's obsessed with her hair."

"Ah, let her be. She's already upset because Justin obviously prefers me over her." As much as I hate Faye, she's still a part of something that shouldn't even exist. If we didn't have to compete, maybe all of us girls could be friends. Okay, maybe not, but we could at least be civil.

This is only my second date since we started the one-on-one dates. Elle is in charge of setting them up, and Joanna told her not to put me with Anders. Unfortunately, Elle said she couldn't do that, but she could put him last on the rotation with me.

"Which means Faye's looking for a new man. She's going out with Nico tonight. Poor guy won't know what hit him."

Nico continued to give girls low scores on their dates, and Katelyn said when she went out with him, they didn't do anything. He took her back to his house, left her in his drawing room alone, and then had a driver bring her home. I feel bad for him. He's grieving and shouldn't be put in this position, but I also understand the girls' point of view. None of it is fair.

I enter the foyer with Faye, Harlow, Abi, and Lexi. Joanna followed me down as well, even though she doesn't have a date tonight. The betas stand in the foyer, and I look for Ryne, but he's nowhere to be seen. Joanna races up to Grady and plants a kiss on his lips. He whispers something in her ear, and she giggles.

I approach them, and she gives me the stink eye. "No hanky panky, you two," she says.

Grady reaches around and wraps an arm around my waist, planting a wet kiss on my cheek.

"Hey," Joanna screeches, and Grady laughs.

"I love making her jealous."

I shove away from him. "Well, I don't. So, hands off."

"Yeah, hands off my girl," Justin yells from behind me. I flush but don't turn around. Faye meets my eyes and glowers at me as she stalks over to Nico. She loops her arm through his, but he shakes her off. If things keep going poorly for Faye, it's only a matter of time until she retaliates. If she's actually the one behind Nova's murder, I'd better watch my back.

We'll be getting a couple of one-on-one dates a week, and I'm dreading the date that's inevitably coming with Anders. But Anders isn't here tonight either, so I push him from my mind and decide to have fun tonight. It's not often in this place that a girl gets to go on a date with a guy just as friends.

"So where are we going?" I ask as we head out to the car. It snowed a little last night, and the day never warmed up enough to melt it off. We get a few snowfalls every year, but something about this one felt different. Maybe because it was my first big storm in the wolf city instead of being bundled up at home with my family in the village.

"How do you like ice skating?" he asks, as if the words should mean something to me.

"What's that?"

Grady stops and turns to me with a boyish grin. "Did I find a sport that the infamous Poppy doesn't know how to do? Hmm, this should be interesting."

Twenty minutes later, we pull up to a massive circular building. I've never seen such a thing before.

He opens the door, and the icy night air greets me. We walk through the doors and the inside of the building isn't much warmer than the outside. We enter a small room lined with shelves full of boots, except these boots have blades on the bottom. Grady takes a pair of white ones off a shelf and holds them out for me to see. "This is an ice skate." He grins like he's discovered gold.

"It looks like a weapon."

He laughs and retrieves a black pair for himself. Sitting on a bench, he shows me how to get the skates on and then helps me up.

When we walk out of the small room, I gasp at the size of the massive space. It's wide open with a shiny white floor.

"What's that?" I ask.

"That's an ice rink, come on."

He pulls me to the edge of the floor and then takes to the ice like a crane landing on water—graceful and smooth. He's obviously done this many times before. Grady does a long turn about the ice and then comes back to teach me. As with all of my other athletic endeavors, I expect this one to come naturally. Five minutes later, I'm flat on my back and realizing it most certainly is not easy.

This ice is rock hard, and my butt kills, but I'm not one to give up, so I climb to my feet and keep trying. I'm terrible, but at least I can say I tried. Grady gives me some tips, and soon I'm doing a decent job—not good—but decent. He skates circles around me as we talk.

"I'm worried about Joanna," I blurt out. I can't help it, and she'll kill me if she finds out, but I can't keep this to myself.

His face falls. "What's wrong?"

I jump right into my theory about Nova's death, that I think she was murdered and that someone might be targeting the fated mates of the betas. Grady's face turns stark white, worry casting a garish hue across his handsome features.

"She's not taking her safety seriously," I finish up, "so I need your help protecting her without her knowing I said anything." I almost tell him about Lexi, but since I don't have irrefutable evidence, I don't want to go accusing her just in case I'm wrong.

"I'll make sure she stays safe." There's an edge to his tone that I know I put there, but I don't feel bad. I'm glad he knows. I need his help.

Voices float across the ice and I spin, nearly falling over in the process.

Two figures appear with skates in hand—Ryne and Elle.

CHAPTER 7

I MANAGE to ease myself to the edge of the rink and lean against the wall, since I can't even stay up on my own two feet. Elle leans into Ryne, and the green-eyed monster rears in my chest. I watch them. I shouldn't, but I do. Ryne seems so easy with her. They laugh and talk like they've known each other for years—which they have—but it seems so odd to see Ryne this happy and relaxed. He's normally brooding and grumpy.

Maybe he's making the right decision. That thought alone breaks my heart into a million razored pieces.

Grady skates up to them, pulling Ryne aside. Elle takes off across the ice like she was born on it. She picks up speed, jumps and spins in the air, and lands gracefully on one skate. Ryne whoops, and she beams.

She meets my eye and glides over to me.

"Poppy, why aren't you skating?" Concern shines in her coppery eyes.

"Because I can't seem to stay upright." I shrug helplessly.

She giggles and holds out her hands. "I'll teach you."

I let her pull me a little ways out.

"How did you learn to jump like that?" I ask.

"Oh, it's freezing all winter in Chicago, so I skate often. It's one of my favorite things. I begged Ryne to find me a place to go. I didn't think I'd be able to skate here. He said as soon as I arrived, he put some wolves on getting this place up and running again. Isn't that sweet?"

She doesn't know about me and Ryne, so she doesn't know about the knife she's twisting. I smile and let it go. She holds tight to my hand as we wobble—correction, I wobble—onto the ice. I think about this rink and what it must have cost to get it fixed up and running again, and compare it to my family at home making do without electricity. Some things really aren't fair.

"I thought you were supposed to be good at anything athletic," she teases, her tone playful. She's impossible not to like.

"I thought so too." I roll my eyes. "Turns out ice doesn't like me."

Elle spins around so she's skating backward and grabs my other hand. At least I can stay upright with her hauling me across the ice, but I feel like a fool.

We pass Ryne and Grady, who are speaking in low voices, both serious. I hope he's not telling Ryne what I told him about Joanna. She's going to be angry enough that I told Grady when she inevitably finds out.

Elle doesn't even look at them as she turns and looks longingly at the ice.

"I think I've got it now. You can go," I offer.

"Are you sure?"

No. I'm going to fall on my butt the second she lets go, but I don't want her to know that. The girl wants to skate, and I'm slowing her down. "Positive."

She nods once and releases my hands. As long as I don't try to move my feet, I'll be fine. I stand there for a few moments, shivering. I have to move, or I'm going to freeze. Maybe I can just go back to the car.

I shuffle my feet forward a few inches and immediately lose my balance. But before I can hit the ice, strong arms catch me. I inhale the woody scent of Ryne and try to keep my composure.

"You're not very good at this, are you?" He keeps one arm tight around my waist, and I try not to notice how much I appreciate his body next to mine.

"No. I think I'm going to ask Grady to take me home."

I twist my head around looking for Grady, but he's gone.

"He's going to take care of Joanna. I told him Elle

and I can get you home. Don't worry, he's still going to give you full points for this date."

"What? Why?" And also, why would he leave me here? Being the third wheel on a date between Elle and Ryne is a special kind of torture.

"Joanna's in danger. Isn't that what you told him? I'm letting him keep her at his house now. She'll come for classes like Nova did during the day, but that's all."

Dread fills my stomach. Joanna is going to kill me. I groan.

"I thought you'd be happy about that," he says.

"I am, and I'm not. Of course, I want her to be safe. But Nova was staying with Nico when she got killed, so it's not like it's a guarantee of safety. And you and I both know Joanna won't like this at all. She's going to be angry that I blabbed."

Ryne doesn't respond. We both watch Elle spin circles for a few moments. Ryne tightens his grip on me. "You're shivering. Come on, I'll take you back to the car. We can wait in there while Elle gets her skating fix in."

I meet his eyes. The electricity between us is undeniable. "Do you really think that's a good idea?"

He swallows. "No. But I'm not going to let you freeze to death either."

He breaks the gaze and shouts out over the rink. "Hey, Elle, we're going to wait in the car."

She waves us on, and he turns me around. We shuffle

to the edge of the rink, change back into our regular shoes, and escape the freezing building. Outdoors is just as cold, but I'm sure Ryne's car is much warmer.

Nerves dance in my stomach. I have no idea what's about to happen. Ryne and I haven't been alone since the night of the brawl.

We near the car, and Knox rushes out to open the back door. He meets my eye but doesn't say anything.

I guess we're not really going to be alone.

But having Knox around won't stop Ryne from doing anything. Ryne might treat Knox with respect, but he's still a slave and a human. And Ryne doesn't know the history between us. Would he keep Knox around if he did?

We slide into the backseat, and I'm immediately grateful for the blast of hot air coming from within. I'm acutely aware of Ryne next to me, but I don't look at him. I pull my hat and gloves off. My braids are a mess, so I untie them and shake out my hair, combing my fingers through the unruly locks. I close my eyes for a second and let out a long sigh of relief. I'm never going ice skating again.

"Knox, do me a favor," Ryne says. "Go take a walk."

My eyes pop open, and I meet Knox's gaze in the rearview mirror. His cheeks are red, and his jaw is set. I've never seen those sweet brown eyes of his looking so dark and heated. He holds me there for a minute, as if daring me to speak up, and then he tears his gaze away and follows Ryne's orders. The door slams, and the alpha prince and I are alone. The temperature in the car rises by ten degrees. Or at least it feels like it does.

"Why'd you send him away like that?" It's a baiting question, but I need to know. I want to hear him tell me all the things I've been longing to hear, like that he can't live without me, and that I'm his fated mate. But those silly ideas are probably all in my head.

Ryne growls low and slides in close, his large frame trapping me against the seat. Everything about having him near feels right.

"I didn't like the way he was looking at you. And I especially didn't like the way you were looking at him."

I shudder and try to deflect because I'm suddenly nervous. As much as I want Ryne, I don't want Knox getting into any trouble because of me. "I wasn't looking at him. I had my eyes closed and was trying to untangle my hair."

I'm such a liar. Can Ryne sense that in me?

"And that's the other reason I sent him away," Ryne responds. "So I could get five minutes alone with you." He reaches up and grips long fingers against my scalp, threading them into my hair and messing it all over again. I'm caught in his hands—in him—and all I can do is stare. His own black hair hangs around his chin. He's still got his beanie on. It's tugged low, framing the stormy blue of his eyes. There's something so completely male about him, so alluring and dangerous, and *mine*. I can't bear to be apart from him for another second. My gaze drifts to his lips. They're a little chapped from the cold.

He growls again—this time I can hear the wolf in him, and then those red lips are on mine.

I sink into him as he pushes me flat on the seat and covers my body with his. He's too tall for it, which makes the space tighter and forces our bodies even closer. If our first kiss was a confession, and our second was a refusal, this one is a promise. He tastes and smells and feels like everything my mama warned me about. But he also feels right, and I can't help from wanting more.

His hands slide under the hem of my shirt to grip my waist, and they are so hot, hotter than a human's, but I like it. It spreads a warmth through me that has nothing to do with the heat and everything to do with instinct. Ryne and I--we are meant to be together. I know it. He knows it. How could either of us deny that? My heart is open to him. It's not smart or logical, but it's the truth, and it fills me with a million wondrous emotions.

His mouth explores mine, and my hands explore him—his arms, his shoulders, his face, his chest, his back

. . .

Someone knocks on the door, giving us just enough warning to pull apart before it opens. Elle pops her head in. Her nose is rosy, and her eyes are round as saucers. She doesn't look shocked. She doesn't even look mad. She looks annoyed.

And hurt.

"You know, Ryne, I didn't come all the way from Chicago for this," she snaps. "And I certainly don't think it's what either of our fathers had in mind when they brokered our betrothal."

Ryne doesn't say a word. He locks eyes with me for one moment more, and then he sits up and peels me away from him. I didn't even realize I was holding onto him until he separates us, and that action alone stings. But that's nothing compared to the pain of the words coming out of Elle's mouth. The pieces have fallen into place, and realizing Ryne's future doesn't include me is like a slap to the face. So much for being his fated. If I were, he wouldn't have even had Elle brought out here. The second he laid eyes on me, he would've called things off with her.

I'm a silly girl who thinks the sexy bad boy wants me. But he's just using me.

"Listen, Elle, I can explain," Ryne finally speaks.

"Save it." She holds up a hand. "You wolves are all the same. I really shouldn't be surprised, but I do have to admit that I expected more from you."

He shakes his head. "But Poppy isn't who you think—"

"This isn't about Poppy." She looks at me for the first time. "I can see why you like her. But the fact is she's not here for you, Ryne. Think about how you're disrespecting your role. You're not a beta. You're an alpha and a prince. I'm a luna from one of the strongest bloodlines in all the wolf cities, and we both know that our fathers will end up battling for alpha king if you and I don't get married and you become the sole heir to that role."

I gulp. There's so much more to unpack here than I could've realized.

"But more than that, we're friends. Maybe think about how you'd feel if you caught me making out with some human in the middle of our date." She raises her eyebrows. "Because I'm not going to go through with this if you're not going to be faithful."

Then she slams the door shut, and the last of my hope slams shut with it.

CHAPTER 8

WE ARRIVE HOME RIGHT before dinner, but I've lost my appetite. The only thing I want is Ryne, as much as I know I shouldn't. Knowing I can't have him only makes me want him more. He consumes my thoughts and fills my body with desire. On the way home, Elle and I sat in the back of the car while Ryne sat up front with Knox.

No one said a word.

I escape to my room and collapse onto my bed. The door bangs open seconds later, and Joanna stomps in.

"Thanks a lot," she says, flinging open the closet door. I sit up and see a suitcase on the floor.

"What's going on?" My mind is a mess from everything that just happened.

She spins on me, her eyes blazing. "You told Grady

that you thought whoever murdered Nova killed her because she stole Nico from us and that I'm next."

I sigh heavily. "Joanna. You weren't taking this seriously. He can protect you better than anyone."

She tosses her dresses into the suitcase and rips open the dresser drawers. "Well, thanks to you, now I'm never going to be let out of his sight. I have to move into his house." Her voice goes low. "I was trying to get you into the Resistance, and now I won't be able to."

I blink at her. "Wait. What? I've been waiting for you to say something about it. I'm ready. I want in."

She shrugs. "Good luck then, because your one and only contact has officially been benched. You know I love Grady, but I really needed this year to figure out some stuff before getting married to him."

"You still can."

"No, I can't. Because Ryne has given Grady permission to take me as his mate at the next moon festival. He doesn't have to wait until the harvest. That's six months early, Poppy."

"You'll be married..." My eyes start to water. I don't want to lose her yet. She was the only thing that made this place bearable.

"He says I can come back here for classes if I want. But I don't know. He sure made it sound like by the time we're married, we won't be leaving each other's sides for the first year, and I won't be interested in classes anyway. I'll probably be pregnant within a few months." Her body goes rigid. "Pregnant! Do you know I never wanted to have children? Who would in this world? What a perfect way to trap me here."

I rub the tears from my eyes. "This wasn't my intent. I only wanted to keep you safe."

"Well, maybe you should think before you speak." She slams the suitcase shut and zips it up. "This ruins everything."

"Really, Joanna, it doesn't. You love him, and he loves you. Some of us would kill for that kind of marriage." The words are out of my mouth before I even realize what I said.

Her eyes narrow. "Well, thanks to you, no one's going to kill me for it." She says it like it's a problem, but I'm not going to apologize for saving her life. I do feel bad about the Resistance stuff though.

She jerks the suitcase off the bed and leaves the room, slamming the door. I don't know if she'll forgive me for this, and I don't have the energy to fight with her. I never want to get out of bed again.

I don't want to think about death and murder, or the Resistance, or any of it.

Instead, I close my eyes and relive the kiss from this afternoon. It was so much better than the ones before, and there is no way Ryne could play our first kiss off as something for Anders's benefit. Or our second kiss as a mistake. This was real. And he was in it as much as I was—as much as I still am.

A soft knock comes at the door. "Come in," I call, not wanting to get up. Elle appears, carrying a tray of sandwiches and chips. She's the last person I expected, and my face immediately warms.

She sets the tray on my dresser. "You didn't come to dinner."

"I didn't feel like facing anyone." I sit up, and she sinks onto Joanna's bed.

"I'm sorry about the outburst in the car. I was. . . disappointed to find Ryne behaving like every other wolf I know. I thought he was better than that."

I curl into a ball and retreat into myself. I don't want to talk about this. Especially not with her. She moves from Joanna's bed to mine and puts an arm around my shoulder. I'm so shocked that I don't even push her away. I want to hate her, but I can't. This isn't her fault.

"I want you to know that I don't blame you at all. For one thing, you couldn't have known about the seriousness of our betrothal. Nothing has been announced, and nobody's told you a thing about our family dynamics. For another, I get it. He's Ryne Tremaine, the alpha prince. No one says no to the alpha prince. I thought he was just being nice to you because your date bailed." She scoffs. "I should've known. I'm sorry." She lets go of me and lies back against the pillows. "I don't even love him. I mean, I think I probably could love him at some point, but I don't. He's too much like a brother. We've never even kissed. But I've known for a while that we were going to get married. You've met the alpha king, right?"

I nod, my body instantly going cold at the thought of Thorn Tremaine. Part of me wants to tell Elle to go away, but another part is totally entranced by her story.

"Well, my father is his second in command and itching to take over. He's nearly challenged Thorn on multiple occasions. He hasn't because there's no guarantee he could win, and it would be a bloodbath. Others would rise to challenge the victor, and it would weaken the entire wolf shifter packs for a while. But he chafes under Thorn's rule. Our mothers actually intervened and proposed the marriage. Of course, neither one of them consulted with me or Ryne. But that's the way of things, I suppose."

I go stiff at that comment, and she frowns. "What's wrong?"

I eye her for a long minute, hoping I can trust her. She has a calming yet powerful energy, and something about that makes me want to be around her. "It's what you said about the way of things. Aren't you tired of it?"

"Of course, I'm tired of it." Intensity sparks in her eyes. "I've had my entire life dictated to me from the moment I was born—from where I went to school and what I could learn, to when I could shift and what I could do. Even down to who I'm going to marry." She takes my hands in hers. They're hot, a reminder of the wolf on the inside. "But as frustrating as that is, I know it's nothing compared to what you girls have to go through, especially the ones who won't get matched with a beta, and I'm sorry."

She's earnest—means every word—and I'm suddenly overcome with the urge to cry and rage all at the same time. Why does she have to be so nice and so perfect for Ryne? I squeeze her hands back. "Elle, we don't need to compare our pain. Yours is just as legitimate as mine, even if it looks different." I'm struck with a thought. I should keep it to myself, but I can't help sharing it. "Are you sure you want to marry Ryne? You said you didn't love him. Don't you want to be with someone you love? And what's more, don't you want to find your fated mate?"

She drops my hands and stands, pacing the floor, her sunshine yellow dress brushing her thighs as she moves. "Of course I want to marry for love or find my fated," she laments. "What's more, I want the freedom to change at will and be my wolf whenever I choose, to hunt and do my duty to the pack in the ways that are denied to me. But there's so many layers to this, and that's what I'm trying to get you to understand." She stops and turns on me, her face growing stern. "I must marry Ryne. If I don't, my father will challenge Thorn, and he'll probably lose. Thorn will destroy my family if that happens. He'll kill us all. My mother, my brothers, and me. And I'll do anything to make sure that doesn't happen."

And now I feel terrible for goading her. "I understand." I swallow hard. "I would do anything to go back and save the family I lost to the wolves. I'd sacrifice my life if I had to."

"We're two sides to the same coin." She smiles sadly before reaching over and grabbing my hand again. "I'm still sorry I caught you with him. It's probably not a good idea for you to fool around with him anymore. I know your date ditched you, but your only chance at a decent life is to fight for a beta, and they won't want a girl who's been with the alpha because then they'll think you belong to him." Her cheeks redden. "They want you to be virgins for the betas. I'm under the same hypocritical rules too."

I look down at my hands, unsure of what to say. I wasn't just fooling around with him, and this isn't about lust. It's so much more—maybe even love, maybe even fate. "What if I do belong to him?" My voice is small. Up until that kiss, I wasn't sure what I felt for Ryne, but now, I feel as if I'll die without him.

She lets out a laugh. "Come on, Poppy, I thought you were smarter than this. Ryne belongs to no one. Don't set yourself up for heartbreak."

Exactly. He belongs to no one, which means he doesn't belong to her either.

I stare at her. I haven't admitted this to anyone. But I haven't been able to make sense of the way I feel, and here is Elle, sweet and open and willing to listen. My words tumble out of my mouth without warning. "I'm not a fool, but there is something about Ryne. I'm drawn to him, and it feels like he's drawn to me too. From the first moment I met him, he hasn't been able to keep his eyes off of me. And when we kiss, everything else falls away."

Her face loses all expression. "What are you saying? Do you think you're his fated mate?" Her voice rises three notches, giving me pause.

"No, nothing like that." I backtrack. Maybe this confession was a bad idea, because what if I am his fated mate? That would change everything, for her included. Either way, I'm not sure I'm ready to confess it to her. I hope she can be trusted, but if there's anything I've learned these past months, it's that the wolves aren't always what they seem.

She continues pacing in front of me. "Good. Because if you were Ryne's fated, he'd have said something by now." Her voice shakes as she speaks, and I can tell she's starting to doubt herself. She's not even looking at me anymore, and she's muttering to herself. "If you were his fated, he would have called off the betrothal. Wolves don't deny their fated mates, Poppy. They just don't. I'm sorry."

She finally looks at me, desperation in her eyes.

"I didn't say that. But there's a lot of chemistry between us, and I like him a lot."

She gives a stiff nod. "Right. Chemistry. It's all lust or physical attraction or whatever. There's no way you're his fated." Her body stiffens, and she faces me with crossed arms and narrowed eyes. "I would appreciate if you stayed away from him now though. You understand what's at stake, right? If I don't marry him, then my whole family will die. Please, Poppy."

I nod even though I don't mean it. Because the more she talks, the less I believe her.

Ryne is my fated.

As much as I want to help save her family, it's impossible for me to stay away from Ryne. I don't even feel like I have a choice anymore. The thought alone makes me sick.

She rushes from the room, and I collapse onto my bed, my emotions swirling with guilt and worry. I already miss Joanna. She'd be able to help me figure this out.

I don't know what's worse--not being Ryne's fated mate or being his mate and still being rejected. And I stupidly confessed my feelings to Elle—the perfect luna who is supposed to marry him. Sure, I denied thinking he was my fated, but I'm pretty sure she saw right through that. I allowed my emotions to be flayed wide open for her judgment. Any other girl in this house would use that against me. All I can do now is pray that Elle isn't like the other girls here.

I groan, pushing my palms into my eyes. What was I thinking?

CHAPTER 9

A SCREAM WRENCHES through the air, and I jerk awake. I look at Joanna's bed, but it's empty. Someone screams again, and I leap from the cocoon of blankets. Where's Joanna? Is she okay? My mind races with images of her floating in the water, her body replacing Nova's. But then reality catches up to me.

She's safe at Grady's house.

But that doesn't explain the screaming.

I wrench open my door to find several other girls have done the same, everyone looking as equally confused and scared as I am. It's dark, and it feels like the middle of the night, but the adrenaline has us all wide awake. My eyes have quickly adjusted to the dark, and I survey the hall, looking for signs of trouble.

The screaming continues, loud and desperate. I'm pretty sure it's coming from Abi and Lexi's room. I rush to their door and stumble inside, flipping on the light. What I find will forever be burned into my brain. Blood is everywhere. Abi sits in the middle of the room, still screaming, her hands and nightdress stained crimson. My eyes scan the room, and I find Lexi's mutilated body on the floor next to the closet. Her throat has been slit, and her face scratched up. I can't even tell definitively if it's Lexi's body, but there's no mistaking that curly black hair. It was her signature, and now it's matted with blood.

Someone pushes past me. Madame Delphine and Madame Vivien stop two steps into the room. Then Madame Delphine grabs Abi by the shoulders. "What happened?"

Abi continues to scream. Madame shakes her and asks again, this time louder. "What happened?"

Abi collapses into Madame Delphine's arms, sobbing incoherently. Madame Vivien looks around the room, and then her eyes land on mine. "Can you tell me what happened?"

Ever since the Wolf Moon Festival, the woman has taken it easier on me, but tonight the edge has returned to her voice and the venom to her eyes. Does she suspect I had something to do with this?

"No. I just got here." I hold up my hands and shake my head. "I have no idea." A few girls crowd in behind me, and several of them begin to cry.

There's no denying Lexi was murdered.

She was never very kind to me, and she'd made enemies with a lot of the claimed in the house with her snooty attitude, but nobody deserves this kind of death. Lexi was easily the smartest girl in the house. She excelled in every subject and was top of the leaderboard. She had so much promise. No wonder she was killed. She was practically guaranteed a beta.

My mind reels with the implications as I stare at her mutilated body, unable to take my eyes off of her. I can't believe I thought she was the murderer. I'm a horrible detective and no closer to finding the killer. Joanna was right. No girl could possibly have inflicted that kind of damage to a body. But a Lycan could.

I step back into the hallway and look around at my fellow claimed, my mind racing through the very real possibility that one of them could be next. I used to look at all of them like suspects, and now I see them as future victims. Someone is after us. The distillery girls huddle together, their faces ashen as they whisper to each other. The rest of the girls appear to be in shock, none of them speaking at all.

I press myself up against the wall and listen when Abi finally speaks. Her voice is so overcome by sobs that it's hard to understand her. "I—I had to go to the bathroom and... and when I came back, I didn't want to turn on the lights and wake up Lexi, so I just came in, but then I tripped over something, and it was her body and…" She's overcome with hysterics, and once again her voice is lost to the horror of it all.

Madame Delphine closes the door, leaving us out here to speculate.

"Did you see the body?" Blair appears next to me. She's one of the distillery girls, and I think this might be the first time she's addressed me personally.

I blink and turn to her. "Yeah."

"Well?" Faye comes to Blair's side and threads her arm through her friend's. "What did it look like? Someone slit her throat."

I open and close my mouth a few times, remembering again exactly what I saw. This wasn't a clean death. "Actually, it looked like Lexi was attacked by a lycan."

"That's impossible," Faye scoffs. "It's not a full moon, you idiot."

"Do you think the lycan can turn on nights that aren't full moons?" Alyssa approaches. At least she doesn't call me an idiot. Everyone is listening to our conversation now, and that question alone increases the tension tenfold.

Faye sends Alyssa a scathing look. "Don't be stupid. Of course, it wasn't a lycan. It had to have been one of us." She turns on me. "You were the first one in there, weren't you, Poppy? Hmm, can you explain why you got there so fast when your room is literally on the other end of the floor?"

I shake my head, unprepared to defend myself.

"That's what I thought." She glares. "Everyone needs to stay away from you. Don't think you're fooling us with this innocent act."

"That's enough, girls." Madame Vivien slips into the hall. Her hands are streaked with blood, and her eyes are rimmed in tears. "Go back to bed. We'll conduct interviews in the morning to see if anyone saw anything. For now, it's best if you don't talk among yourselves anymore. We wouldn't want anyone's stories to get tainted by false information."

We disperse, but I can still hear Faye whispering. "See, they definitely think it was one of us."

She's going to convince them all to turn on me, that's if she hasn't already done so. I can feel it deep down to my center. Maybe I should have gone to stay with Joanna and Grady. Maybe I still can. This whole time I was worried about Joanna getting targeted, and now Lexi is dead. If that's the case, that any of us could be murdered, then I need to be extra careful. Everyone here hates me.

But I don't need to worry about being blamed for this one by anyone who saw the body. Everyone who stepped in that room knows the truth as well as I do. How could a human girl do that to someone in such a short amount of time? Answer: she couldn't. There isn't a girl in this house who could inflict deadly wounds with claws and teeth. And if a lycan couldn't have been here since it's not the full moon, then there's only one reason-able explanation.

A wolf did this.

I lie awake for hours. There is no way I can sleep after seeing Lexi's body. What wolf would want her dead and why? I think about all the times I saw Lexi with one of the betas. She always stayed near them but was never overbearing like Faye. Her single dates had been with Anders and Justin.

Justin wouldn't do this. He was too nice.

But Anders.

Maybe.

The question still remains as to why. Not to mention that he'd have to sneak in here in the middle of the night and risk getting caught. She went on a date with him ages ago, so if she did something to make him mad, this would've been a delayed reaction.

I roll over and punch the pillow. Sleep will never come for me now. I sit up and flick on the light, grabbing the book about roses that Justin's mom gave me, trying to read it. I understand most of the words, but some of the bigger ones still elude me. It's not exciting, but at least I'm not constantly picturing Lexi's blood all over the place. I read for an hour or so and then peek outside my window. It's still dark, but maybe I can go for a run.

I shiver.

Whoever killed Lexi might still be out there. I think I'll wait for daylight hours and company. But I can't stay in my room anymore. I want to crawl out of my skin. Instead I head for the showers. I'll have to take another one after we workout, but at least I can get out of my room.

I push open the door to hear sobbing coming from one of the stalls.

"Hello," I call, but no one responds. I find the stall where the crying is coming from. "Are you okay?"

Whoever is in there continues to cry. I pull the shower curtain back an inch and peek in. Abi is sitting on the floor in the corner, her limp black hair hanging in sheets around her face. She's curled into a tiny ball, and I can't see her face, but her whole body is shaking. She's still wearing her bloodstained nightgown, and water pours from the showerhead. She's sopping wet but doesn't seem to notice or care.

I sink down onto the floor and wrap my arms around her tiny frame. She jerks her head up and then collapses into me. I hold her while she cries, and eventually she pulls away and wipes at her face. Her wide almond eyes are rimmed red, and her lips are puffy.

"I . . . I . . . I'm sorry," she says, her breath still heaving.

"It's okay. If that had been Joanna, I'd be a mess too."

"They took her body away, and Madame Vivien

helped me clean up the blood, but they wanted me to just sleep there. I couldn't."

"Of course you couldn't. Listen, Joanna isn't staying in my room anymore. You can stay there. You don't ever have to go back into that room again. If you want, I'll even go get your clothes and stuff for you."

She nods, but her gaze is unfocused.

"How long have you been here?" I ask.

She shrugs. "I don't know. A while."

"You need sleep. Come on."

I help her up and back to my room. I get her clothes and even help her change. She falls onto Joanna's bed, and I tuck her under the covers. She starts to cry again, so I climb in with her and hold her until she falls asleep. Once she's settled, I extract myself from her and sit back on my own bed. I really do want a shower, but I don't want to leave Abi alone. She looks so small and broken.

If Joanna had been the one murdered, would anyone have been as nice to me?

I seriously doubt it.

But this isn't about me, and I realize I've been so wrapped up in my drama with Ryne that I've lost focus on what's important. These girls need my help. I don't know how, but one way or another, I'm going to find a way to save them.

CHAPTER 10

THE DOOR FLINGS open early the next morning, and Joanna bounces in. "You are totally forgiven," she announces. "Grady's bed is the most comfortable place I've ever slept in my life."

I raise my eyebrows at her. "Grady's bed?"

She climbs into my bed and smacks me on the shoulder. "Shut up. But yeah." Her face flushes. This is the first time I've ever seen her embarrassed. Are the rules different because Joanna and Grady are fated? Probably.

"Don't tell anyone, okay?" she whispers. "I don't want them to ruin this for me."

I understand because I'd feel the same way in her position. "So what happened? Did you, you know?" I ask in a hushed voice, raising my eyebrows.

"We're going to wait until the wedding, but we still

fooled around a little," she admits with a wide smile. "I can't help myself, Poppy. He's too perfect."

"I'm happy for you."

She rolls onto her back, and I spot a necklace I've never seen her wear before. "What's that?" I ask. It's got a pretty gold chain with a white jeweled heart.

Joanna's fingers fly to it. "Oh, it's from Grady. It was his mom's."

My eyes flick over to her bed where Abi still sleeps. In spite of Joanna's noise, she hasn't stirred. Either that, or she's pretending to sleep while listening, but I don't think so. Abi isn't the type.

Joanna follows my gaze. "You've replaced me already?"

She pulls a bag out of her pocket and offers me a piece of red candy. I shake my head. "Something happened last night," I confess. "Something bad."

I tell her about Lexi's murder and everything I saw. Her face goes ashen, and her hands shake as I tell the story. "She had to have been targeted," I conclude, cuddling into Joanna's side and wishing she could somehow wipe my memory so we didn't have to have this conversation. "There's no other explanation for Lexi being killed like that."

Joanna finally speaks, her voice much calmer than her trembling hands. "So someone must have been waiting in or near the house, watching for Abi to leave Lexi alone in the room. Then he went in there, shifted into his wolf, ripped her throat out, and then left before anyone saw him."

"That's what I think. As much as I wish it weren't true, it's the only thing that makes sense."

"And he was fast, too," Abi's scratchy voice filters from across the room. She rolls over, stretching her arms over her head and wiping at her puffy eyes. "I couldn't have been gone for more than four or five minutes."

We all sit up and stare at each other from across the room. "Did you see anything weird lately with Lexi?" I ask.

Next to me, Joanna's hands continue to tremble. She brushes her hair out of her face but doesn't say anything.

Abi shakes her head. "I dunno, maybe. Lexi mostly kept to herself. I didn't hang out with her enough to know if something was going on. We were only room-mates, you know?"

Abi's one of the wannabe distillery girls who's been trying, and failing, to get in with Faye's crew. I wonder what she thinks about being in here with me. Maybe she'll act like Charlotte did and ditch me the first chance she gets.

"What about Samantha? Do you think she'd know anything?" Samantha is Lexi's best friend in the house.

Abi shakes her head. "She and Samantha had a falling out recently. I would suspect she had something to do with it if I hadn't seen the evidence of a wolf attack."

The sun brightens through the windowpane, and there's no more time to chat. We get dressed in our workout gear and head out for our morning exercises. Joanna's movements are jumpy, and she keeps a close eye on Abi.

"You okay?" I ask as we tromp down the stairs behind everyone else. No one will get close to Abi now.

"What? Yeah. Of course I am."

I nudge her. "Is this about last night at Grady's? Did something else happen?"

She sighs dramatically. "Nothing happened beyond what we talked about. I told you I'm fine."

She moves in front of me and shoves a few other girls out of the way. She's not fine, but I don't know what her problem is. She's probably still thrown off by Lexi's death. We all are. I loop my arm through Abi's, and she gives me a forced smile.

I wonder if Madame Vivien is going to go easy on me, or if she'll single me out again like she did after Charlotte turned. Or maybe she'll go after another unsuspecting victim.

But she's not there.

Ryne is.

No betas. No madames. Only the alpha.

"Ladies, please take a seat on the grass. No talking among yourselves. You're welcome to exercise if you'd like or sit and relax. Please spread out so you aren't near anyone else. I'm going to be personally conducting interviews regarding Lexi's death."

Ryne's expression is guarded, but I can see that his eyes are haunted and tired. If there's nobody else here to conduct interviews, that must mean he's considering everyone to be a suspect. This must be hard on him. I want to go to him and comfort him, but that's Elle's job. She's not here either.

I lie flat on the grass and stare up into the blue sky. It's cold, but spring is fast approaching, and with only a few months until the next festival, I know I should be focusing on the leaderboard and the betas. But it's like my body is attuned to Ryne. Even though I'm not watching him, I can feel as he walks from girl to girl, sitting down with them to quietly discuss what they know of last night.

Eventually, he sits next to me. The tips of our fingers touch, not enough for anyone to notice, but enough to send my mind spinning.

"Can you tell me about what you experienced last night?" His voice is gentle, and I look over to meet his eyes. This is the man who kissed me so passionately and then acted like I meant nothing the second his intended opened the car door. I should be angry with him. No, I *am* angry with him. I snatch my hand away and fold it over my chest, then tell him everything he wants to know.

"How can you be sure it was a wolf?" he asks.

"Because her throat was ripped out, and her face was all scratched up. She looked exactly like the girls who were killed by the lycans. Well, not exactly. This seemed a little more controlled."

"Someone could've tried to make it look like a wolf attack."

"But Abi said it was fast, less than five minutes. If someone was trying to make it look like that, they'd have to take more time."

"Unless it was Abi," he retorts.

I sit up and look him straight in the eyes, ready to argue that there is no way Abi did it, but as I meet the stormy blue, I lose my words. Both my mind and my body betray me. I want nothing more than to climb into his lap and feel him press up against me. I want to kiss those lips and run my fingers through his unruly hair.

I want him to ask about us or to give me any indication that he feels the same feelings I do. But he drops his eyes.

"Is there anything else you saw?" he asks.

I fling myself back onto the ground, knowing if I keep looking at him, I'll do something stupid.

"No. That was it. It was a wolf. I know it."

He drops down next to me and brings his lips right up to my ear. "I believe you. But be careful who you share that with." He stays there for a brief moment, his breath hot on the side of my face.

Then he's gone, leaving me for the next girl.

CHAPTER 11

ELLE SITS across from me at the table. After Ryne finished interrogating us, he sent us on a quick run around the field and then straight on to breakfast. He kept his eyes on me the whole time, and I couldn't help but look back. I don't even care if anyone notices my feelings anymore, least of all him. He should know how I feel and be held accountable for leading me on. But now he's gone, replaced by the watchful eye of Madame Delphine. The girls are quiet, most staring blankly into their breakfasts. I stir the oatmeal around listlessly.

"I heard you found Lexi," Elle addresses Abi in a tender voice.

Joanna stiffens. "So?" she says accusingly, jumping in to defend Abi.

It doesn't faze Elle one bit. She keeps her compassionate gaze locked on Abi and continues. "So, that must've been hard for Abi."

Abi stiffens next to me, and I look over. Tears slip from her eyes. She hasn't stopped crying all morning. I hand her my napkin to use as a tissue, and she takes it from me. She's a pretty girl with lovely Asian features, and I hate to see her so upset. But I don't blame her, nor do I judge her. She could cry for days and days, and I'd understand. I did the same thing when Willow died. Growing up, we weren't strangers to death, and it was always sad. But to see it happen violently with my own two eyes—to smell the blood and hear pleading screams snuffed out? That's different. It changes a person forever.

Faye comes over and sits next to Elle, twirling her auburn hair around her finger as if it's any normal morning. She's never sat with us before, and I immediately suspect her motives. Elle gives her a tight smile. I expect Joanna to say something snarky, but she doesn't. I want to get her alone so she can tell me what's going on with her because she's definitely been acting strange ever since she found out about Lexi. I think she knows something.

"Everyone thinks you and Abi killed Lexi." Faye looks right at me, daring me to argue with her.

Abi gasps and collapses into sobs again.

"What are you talking about?" I ask, putting an arm around Abi.

"Oh, don't play stupid. I saw you leave the room. You two were in on it together."

"That's not what happened." This is so ridiculous. I can't believe she thinks those accusations will stick.

"Oh really? Because Lexi was about to land Cade, and you couldn't stand it. And Abi has always been jealous of her." By this point, several of the distillery girls are standing behind Faye as if to back her up. "You're both going down."

I want to jump in and tell them that they're wrong, that it was a wolf who did it, but I remember what Ryne asked and force myself to keep my mouth shut. Abi peels herself from my arms and sprints from the room, Elle and Joanna following close behind. I know they want to make sure she's okay, but I'm left here with no backup.

I stack their plates on my own and stand to carry everything to the kitchen.

"What?" Emma steps in front of me to block my path. "Aren't you going to defend yourself?"

I try to move past her, but she won't let me.

"She can't," Joy interjects. "She knows she's guilty." They're surrounding me on all sides now. The only way to get past would be to shove them, which is probably what Faye wants. She knows how to provoke me. I close my eyes and count to ten.

"We're not going to let you get away with this," Blair adds. "We already told Ryne everything."

That does it. My eyes pop open. "It wasn't me," I snap. "And it wasn't Abi. And Ryne knows it."

"Hmm—well, I guess we'll see about that," Faye says. "You know, someone really ought to warn the betas about you, Poppy."

That makes my cheeks go hot. I hadn't thought of that. I know Ryne will believe me, but what if these girls are successful in poisoning the betas against me?

"Why do you hate me so much?" I'm shaking now. A fork clatters to the hardwood.

But I think I already know the answer. It's because they can tell there's a strong connection between me and Ryne, and Faye has sensed it since the first day. That and she's a bully who recruits other bullies. They want to take everyone else down so that all the distillery girls get to stick together and end up as the beta wives. If the alpha likes me, there's a good chance he'll save me from the mating houses. Faye can't have that.

Right as Faye's about to open her mouth to answer, Madame Delphine sweeps into the room. "Alright, girls," she announces, "it's time to move on to your chores, and then we'll start the lessons. Don't bother changing out of your workout gear into your dresses though," she adds. "Today we're having a special combat session downstairs in the gym."

We disperse, and my mind whirls. Part of me is still caught up in the altercation I just had, but the other part of me is thinking ahead to the future. After Charlotte died, I argued with the shifters about our combat training but had been stonewalled. Truth is, we haven't been learning enough. We don't only need to know hand-to-hand combat. We need to know how to use weapons. We can't properly protect ourselves and can't count on others to do it for us.

We need to learn how to fight off lycans . . . and wolves.

Last night proved it.

<hr>

As we take our positions in the gym, I study the betas with new eyes. One of them probably killed Lexi. Sure, it could've been any wolf, but the more I think about it, the more I think it was one of our betas. Who else knows the manor like the betas? Who else even knew Lexi? It only makes sense that it would've been one of them, and now I want to figure out who it is before they do it again.

Of course, my first thought is Anders. Even though he hasn't been around much lately, I still wouldn't put it past him. But that could just be because I hate him, and I know how violent he can be. I can't let my prejudice cloud my judgment if I'm going to find the killer.

Fact is, all these men are trained killers.

Every. Single. One.

So who was it and why? Did Lexi know something

she shouldn't have? Did she see something? Do something?

"Poppy! Pay attention!" Ryne snaps, and I shake myself into the present. A few of the girls snicker, and I make sure to send him a glare that he promptly ignores. We're lined up along one side of the gym, in front of a myriad of silver weapons laid out on the floor.

Ryne clears his throat. "As I was saying, it takes incredible skill to kill a lycan. Bullets are mostly useless. While they are in their monster form, the only way to kill them is to sever the head from the body." He paces across the room. "You may have heard rumors that silver can kill them." Most of us nod in agreement. "Don't believe everything you hear. Silver will burn them, and if pierced with silver, it can sometimes turn them back into a human—their weakest state—but it doesn't kill them. You need to physically separate the head from the body to do that." I grimace, and he continues. "The best way to kill them is while they're in their human form, which is why we always have units out looking for their camps. They don't stay in one place for long and are excellent at staying hidden, but we've got trackers out there at all times." He nods in the direction of the wilderness, and I shiver.

What must it be like for the lycanthropes? Does the sickness affect them during the other phases of the moon or just the full moons? And most of all, I wonder if Charlotte is still out there in the wilds somewhere, living her new life in a hidden encampment.

"Wolfsbane is poisonous to their kind, making them sick. It's another tool we can use against them, which is why our kind grows it in mass quantities up north." He stops and stares us down, lifting a dried purple flower between his fingers. "It doesn't grow in our soil, so we don't have that advantage here. Never underestimate a lycan. They heal faster than shifters. They're bigger and stronger and bloodthirsty. If you are fortunate enough to weaken one, do not hesitate to kill it."

Ryne hands the dried wolfsbane to Elle, tosses a long sword to Grady, then picks up another and lunges for him. Joanna jerks forward, but I grip her arm and pull her back. Elle grabs her other side. "Let me go," Joanna growls.

"No, watch," I say, pointing at them. They dance around each other with the swords. "He's showing us how they work. Ryne's not going to hurt Grady."

Joanna calms, and we watch them, mesmerized by their violent dance. It's almost elegant, the way they move, but there's an aggression there that I wouldn't want to be on the other side of. Eventually, Grady gains the upper hand and flings the sword out of Ryne's grip. Grady lowers his own sword and steps back.

Ryne hunches over, breathing hard, and then claps Grady on the shoulder. "As you can see, Grady is my swordsman. He has bested anyone he's ever taken on.

He's beheaded his share of lycans as well. He'll be showing you how to use the sword. Anders has the axe, Justin the pair of long daggers, Nico is best with a bow and arrow, and Cade will show you how to throw stars. Once we are comfortable with your skill levels with the weapons, you will all be given one to sleep with. We don't want any of you vulnerable again."

For about an hour, they have us test the various weapons. I do best with the sword and the axe, and I'm awful at the stars.

Ryne gathers us all back together. "You'll train in all weapons, but you'll start with the ones you're strongest in."

My hand shoots in the air.

"Yes, Poppy?" he says slowly.

"If a lycan can only be killed by decapitation, then why are we using some of these smaller weapons?"

He studies me for a second. "Close hand-to-hand combat will be useful for you. No more questions." He walks away.

I frown at his back, then go with Faye, Harlow, Samantha, and Blair to learn swords with Grady. I'm not all that crazy about being in a group with Faye, but at least I didn't have to be in Anders's group.

"I didn't hear Ryne call your name," I say to Elle.

She smirks. "I'm a house mother here, remember? Plus, I already know how to wield all those weapons."

Of course she does. I try not to get any more jealous than I already am of her. "What's your favorite?"

"The daggers. But against a lycan, I'd rather wield an axe."

Exactly. She just made my point.

Some of the weapons we're learning don't make sense with his lecture about the lycans. Because Ryne isn't only worried about lycans attacking us. Of course not. It was a wolf who killed Lexi. Maybe our enemies are more widespread than I know. Besides, I overheard Ryne tell his father that he wanted to expand into panther shifter territory. I don't know how many species of shifters are out there, but I'd wager there are more than wolves and panthers.

The thought strikes me that perhaps one of them killed Lexi, but then I shake it away. That wouldn't make sense. Why would any of them care about her? Or Nova, for that matter.

The fact that Ryne is arming us all makes me feel a little better. It means he doesn't necessarily believe it was one of us girls who is to blame. I hope he's finally taking my pleas for help seriously.

Grady goes over basic sword handling and maneuvering. He gives us sticks to practice with and then puts us in pairs. Since there is an odd number, he partners with Harlow and pairs me with Faye, which I cannot figure out because he knows I can't stand her.

He hands me a stick and leans over to whisper in my ear. "Kick her ass."

I grin. I'm going to be better than her, and he knows it.

Grady backs up and stiffens, dropping the rest of the sticks he's holding, and shoving roughly past me. I spin to see him rushing for Anders's group, where he's teaching the girls how to wield an axe. Anders is fighting with one of the girls, axes in hand, and my stomach tightens. It's Joanna, and he's much stronger than she is. If he's not careful, he's going to kill her.

Grady jumps between Anders and Joanna, knocking the axe out of Anders's hand. It falls to the floor with a metallic thud. "What are you trying to do?" he accuses. Everyone in the room freezes and turns to watch. The energy is thick with aggression—wolves are close at hand.

"You really think that if she goes up against a lycan, they are going to go easy on her?" Anders spits. "I'm trying to teach her to be strong and fight."

"That won't happen if you kill her first."

His words hang as heavy as the axes, and the room goes silent.

CHAPTER 12

"YOU'RE BOTH RIGHT," Ryne interjects, striding to stand between them. "Anders needs to be careful with the women, especially a fated mate like Joanna." He glares at the man. "It would be wise to remember your strength and keep your temper in check."

I scoff. If only Anders had managed that on the harvest day, Willow would still be alive.

"And you." Ryne points to Grady. "You need to stop coddling your mate and stop assuming everyone is out to get her. If you really believe she's a target, then why not get her prepared to fight off anyone who could hurt her? You and I both know you're not always going to be there to protect her."

The men are practically dripping with anger, but they nod and bow their heads to their alpha. Then everything goes back to normal, or as much as it can after that outburst. Maybe stuff like that is normal in the pack, but it's not normal to me. Arguments always had a way of stirring up trouble back home, and I wonder if the same will happen among the betas. As we go back to training, I can't stop thinking about what just happened. This place is brutal. Back home, nobody died from lycan attacks, and we certainly didn't need to train in weapons, but we were told that we needed the shifters' protection against the lycans. Maybe they simply took care of it, and I took it for granted.

I turn back to Faye, my priority shifting to knocking the snot out of her with this stick. I guess this place has rubbed off on me more than I thought.

I raise an eyebrow. "Are you ready?"

She doesn't even bother to answer before diving forward and knocking me on the shins. I wince, falling to my knees. I don't have time to worry about the pain. I whip my stick up, misjudging where she is.

Her stick flies at my face, but I roll out of the way right as it swishes past me and cracks against the gym floor. I kick out, using my combat training to swipe her off her feet. We're on the ground in a tumble of sticks and punches and grunts. I jab the end of my stick into her stomach, and she screams, then bobs her head toward me and bites my arm. Actually bites me!

"Are you crazy?" I scream, ripping my arm away from her. Blood beads along the wound. She spits the blood out with a sadistic grin. Okay, I'm done going easy on her. I jump up, but so does she. We circle each other. In my periphery, I can tell people are watching, but they're nothing to me. All my focus is on Faye.

Faye, who tried to get me sent to the mating house.

Faye, who's treated me and so many others like garbage from day one.

Faye, who said my sister was a whore who deserved to die.

Anger burns inside, growing to an inferno, and I lash out with a battle cry. Her eyes widen, and she screeches, stumbling back. I swing my stick forward, prepared to take her down and take her out, but someone catches it.

Justin.

"Alright, you two." He laughs, as if this whole thing is hilarious. "Settle down. We wouldn't want anyone getting hurt."

I'm not sure if he's protecting me because of our recent date or Faye because they've been all over each other on more than one occasion. Either way, I couldn't care what Justin thinks at this moment. Faye is going down.

I jerk my stick from his hands and nod to Faye. "You giving up?"

She scoffs. "No. I'm not scared of you."

"Then let's fight." I glare at Justin. "It's wood. We're not going to kill each other. We need to learn, like your alpha said." I search for Ryne, but he's deep in conversation with Anders and not paying attention to us. All the better.

Justin shakes his head, "Nope, not on my watch."

"You're not our group leader. Grady is." I use my free hand to brush the hair that fell from its braid out of my face.

"Do you see Grady anywhere?" He looks around, and I notice that he's gone. So is Joanna. Go figure.

I throw my stick to the ground. "Fine. Whatever."

Faye laughs. "Why do you always have to be so dramatic?" She bats her eyelashes at Justin. "She's always like this. If you want to know who causes the most problems in the house, look no further. Not to mention, she's obviously dangerous. I'm pretty sure she wants to take all the girls out. You heard about Lexi, right?"

"I'm not listening to your garbage," I argue. "I'm finding a new weapon."

I turn to survey the weapons training happening all around me. All the while, my hands are shaking, and my heart is pounding. I'm so angry I could scream, but I can't. If all I can do is throw weapons around, then so be it. Elle had said the daggers weren't the best for lycans, but if I can cut one with silver daggers, then I could weaken it enough to kill it, right? And anyway, I could certainly use it if someone comes to kill me in my sleep. Since Justin seems to have given up on the daggers to take over for Grady, I head over to Elle.

I catch her eye and hold up the daggers. They're thin and about as long as my hand, reminding me of sharpened nails. "I'm all yours now," I say. "Teach me your ways."

Elle laughs, but we get to work. The entire time I can feel Ryne watching us. I'm kind of proud of myself though. One, for not watching him back. Two, for walking away from the situation with Faye instead of letting her provoke me further in front of everyone. And three, for staying down here at all. Because there had been a moment when I wanted to walk away, to storm from the gym and take the point deduction for the day.

The old Poppy would've done just that, but I'm trying to be better these days. I need to keep my head on straight and my emotions in check if I'm going to figure out who this murderer is. I need to find them. Because if I don't, it's very possible I could be next.

That night, Abi shuts our door as soon as we go to bed.

"I know who killed Lexi," she blurts.

"What? How?"

"I didn't realize it until today. Like, I don't know. I was a bitch, and I never paid much attention to Lexi, right? Anyway, after her date with Cade, she came home crying and said he'd taken advantage of her. Of course I didn't ask how or why. I was tired, so I told her to go to bed and stop making so much noise." Abi chokes out a sob and covers her mouth. I stand and wrap her in a tight hug, waiting for her to calm down.

She sucks in a few breaths. "I was so horrible to her."

We sit down on the bed, and once her breathing slows, I ask her the most important question. "Why do you think Cade killed her?" Because honestly, Cade hasn't come across my radar at all. He's a flirt, but he always seemed harmless to me. But now that I know he took advantage of Lexi, my opinion of him sours. Did he rape her? I still didn't follow why he would've killed her over something like that, but maybe there was more to the story.

"Isn't it obvious? She was probably going to tell Ryne about what happened. I didn't think about it until Bailey mentioned today that if a beta has sex with one of the claimed before they're married, then he's exiled."

My mouth pops open. I didn't know that. I know we are supposed to stay virginal and that the wolves get to be hypocrites about sex. I know that the king acts like he is above the rules. I know he wants me to be sent to a mating house, and when that didn't happen, he roughed Faye up. "Are you sure that's one of the rules?"

She nods vigorously. "Yeah, Bailey found some old book about it in the library. That's when I put it all together. Don't you see? We're supposed to be virgins for the beta who picks us, just in case of possible pregnancies. They don't want to risk anything happening with their little heirs."

This news makes my stomach lurch. I think I'm going to be sick.

Because of my instant connection to Ryne, I've allowed myself to be blinded to many of the atrocities happening here. I'm embarrassed by my behavior and decide I need to talk to Joanna again. She said she's out of the Resistance now that she's staying with Grady, but I wonder how much of that is true. Maybe she could at least point me in the right direction. A thought strikes me. *Maybe that direction is here in this house...*

"What happens to the girl?" I ask softly.

"She's ruined. They send her to a mating house."

My hands fist into angry balls. "Then Lexi had no incentive to tell Ryne." I hate to say it, but it's true. A woman would be forced to keep quiet or risk losing her chances at a somewhat normal life. And the wolves? I'm sure they know that. Cade could've easily taken advantage.

"Cade didn't care what he did to her." Abi's voice goes hard. "Lexi wasn't the type to sweep something like that under the rug. What if she confronted him? He would've done anything to avoid being exiled, even killing her to keep her mouth shut."

A sinking feeling settles into my stomach.

I bet she's right.

"We have to tell Ryne," I say.

She clutches at me. "We can't."

"Why not?"

"Because if he doesn't believe us, then Cade will come after us next."

"If Cade killed Lexi, do you think he killed Nova as well?"

She nods. "That night at the festival, when Nova left, Cade left too. I remember because I was dancing with him, and he cut us off right in the middle of the song. I didn't think of it at the time, but now it makes sense. What if he tried to start something with Nova? He saw she was alone, and he wanted a taste, and when she resisted, he killed her."

I don't know if it's true, but her story adds up. Either way, he's dangerous.

I squeeze her hand. "Don't worry. We won't let him get away with this."

CHAPTER 13

BEFORE WE CAN GO to Ryne, Abi makes me promise to find solid proof first. She's terrified about retaliation and wants to lie low. Her guilt over what happened puts her into a terrible depression, and her scores fall a little more every day. I'm worried about her, but I don't know what to do. The full moon comes and goes without any incidents, which kind of feels like a miracle. Then we're back to classes and dating.

Tonight I'm scheduled to go on a one-on-one date with Anders.

I've spent the entire day terrified of what could happen with him. When it's time, I get dressed in the most modest outfit I can find. It's a casual date, so I'm in loose jeans, boots, and a heavy wool sweater. It's not quite weather appropriate for the sunny days we've been having, but it'll have to do. It's almost time to go downstairs to meet him when a knock sounds on the door, and Madame Delphine peeks her head in. "Poppy, can I talk to you for a minute?"

It must have something to do with Anders. My heart races as I lead her inside. Abi sits up from where she's lying on the bed. "I'll leave," she says, and then scurries out the door.

"This won't take long," Madame Delphine turns to me. "I'm sorry, but Anders is indisposed. He won't be able to take you on a date. As this isn't your fault, it won't affect your scores."

I plop onto the bed, relief flooding me. Anders is the only beta that's been gone more often than not, and I wonder what could be so important. Maybe all this dating is boring him, and he'll show up at the harvest and select from who's left. Wouldn't that be something?

"I'm sorry. You must be disappointed," she continues, but even I can hear the sarcasm in her voice. It's no secret I hate the guy.

I smile up at her, suppressing a little laugh. "This is the best news I've heard all month."

She waves me away and heads to the door.

"Madame Delphine, can I ask you something?"

She turns to me with curious eyes. I don't wait, don't let myself chicken out. I've been wanting to have this conversation and haven't had an opportunity. "What can you tell me more about the Resistance?"

She freezes, her expression tightening. "Don't speak of it," she hisses low. "Never speak of it."

"Someone has to," I retort. "It's real, isn't it?"

She holds up her hand to stop me. "I have an idea. Why don't you and Abi go outside and find a place for those poppies you're growing in the greenhouse. They should be ready to be replanted."

And with that, she's gone, the door banging closed behind her.

"That was weird," I grumble to myself.

It was also stupid. What if she can't be trusted? But I don't know, my gut keeps telling me she can. I go to the door and find Abi waiting in the hall. "Come on," I say, "let's go plant some flowers."

Hours later, when our work is done, we stand arm in arm and survey it with pride. The little green sprouts litter the entire area next to the woods. There's room for them to grow here, and hopefully spread their seeds through the field. The sepals protect the red buds as the soft wind tests them in their new homes, blowing them gently. I can't wait to see them bloom into magnificent flowers, and I hope it happens soon. The next festival is coming up, and if there's anything I know about festivals, it's that nothing is guaranteed. I may not be around to see the flowers after that. Abi pulls me into a hug—she's probably thinking the same thing.

Before we know it, more days pass, and we're halfway to another full moon. But tonight we don't need to worry about the moon. Tonight, we need to worry about more one-on-one dates. I'm hoping I've dodged Anders for good. I'm also hoping I'll be able to do some more digging around about Nova and Lexi's deaths. So far, I haven't been able to find any evidence on Cade, and I'm growing frustrated.

And worried.

I look over to my new roommate, who has quickly become another best friend, taking Joanna and me from a duo to a trio. "I'm sorry you're going out with Cade tonight," I say to Abi, trying to be cryptic because Joanna is in the room. She's flipping through the dresses in her closet as if she doesn't have a ton of great options to wear. She does, but no dress will make her feel comfortable with that man.

She scoffs but keeps her voice light. We haven't told anyone about her suspicions yet, not even Joanna. I hate keeping secrets from her, but she's closer than ever with Grady, and I don't want her to slip up and say the wrong thing.

"Yeah, I'm nervous," Abi confesses. "We already know he's handsy, and he likes to kiss all the girls, and that's in public. I'm worried about what he'll do in private."

Our thoughts travel to poor Lexi, and we grimace.

"I'm pretty sure you're the only one he hasn't kissed," she adds.

Joanna snorts from where she's lying on my bed. "He hasn't kissed me." She stands and walks over to me. I'm trying to do my hair, but it's not going so well. The humidity has started to come back with the sunshine, and my curls aren't cooperating. She takes the brush from me and immediately snags it on a knot. I wince as she tugs it. She's dressed in a pretty blue sundress with a thin white sweater. It's new. In fact, we all have new dresses for the spring season.

I jerk my head away and snatch the brush out of Joanna's hand so I can get the knot out myself without being reduced to tears. Abi gives up on the closet and slumps down on the bed. For a minute she doesn't say anything. "I don't know why I have to go out with any of them. Everyone knows I'm heading to the mating house at the Pink Moon Festival."

I whip around. "What are you talking about?"

"Ever since Lexi died, I can't seem to concentrate on anything. I'm at the bottom of the board."

Since we've had more combat training, and I'd finally mastered reading, I've been dead smack in the middle of the board and I haven't been paying attention to the last few slots. I feel bad that she's at the bottom, but I'm not sure how to help her. Everyone keeps saying the Pink Moon Festival is supposed to be fun. It's done outside in a garden, and everyone welcomes in the spring by dressing in pastels and dancing around barefoot on the grass. But I can't imagine it being fun when my friend is going to end up shipped off to a mating house by the end of it.

"Don't worry. We've gotten Poppy out of the bottom. We can do it for you too," Joanna says encouragingly, grabbing a dress out of Abi's closet. "Wear this one. Cade likes green."

Abi grabs the dress absentmindedly and disappears out the door to go shower. "How do you know Cade likes green?" I ask.

She snorts. "I don't. But that dress shows off quite a bit of her cleavage, and I know Cade will appreciate that."

I want to scream, because that's the last thing Abi needs, but Joanna doesn't know what I know. So I let it go, trusting Abi to make her own choices. After we finish getting ready, we head down the stairs. I'm not nervous about my date with Nico. A handful of girls have been out with him since Nova died, and they all said basically the same thing—that he took them to his house and left them with his housekeeper to eat dinner. Then he'd bring them back and give them full points. At least he's stopped giving zero points, so I won't mind the leg up on the board.

I wonder if he'll even choose anyone at the harvest moon. Is it possible to back out?

Nico meets me at the door. He's wearing a black suit,

including a black shirt and tie. He is handsome, but in a different way than Ryne. He's thin with an angular face and curly chestnut hair. He keeps the sides shaved, but it's long on the top, so hair is always falling into his stormy gray eyes. His complexion is the opposite of Anders, but now that I know the relation, I can't help but see the resemblances. They have the same build, the same face structure, and even some of the same mannerisms.

He gives me a forced smile and holds out his arm. "Shall we?" he asks.

I nod and glance over at the other girls. Joanna greets Grady with a long kiss, and Cade can't keep his eyes off of Abi's cleavage. She wore the green dress. Anders is with Faye, and Justin looks uncomfortable with Bailey, who won't even meet his eyes.

Nico and I get into a waiting car. This one is smaller than Ryne's but prettier. It's bright red and all curves. Nico drives, and I kind of want to learn. What was it like for Knox to learn to drive? I wish he and I could actually have a conversation about it. I wish I could have a conversation with him about anything, for that matter.

"I thought you all had drivers," I say, running my fingers along the smooth leather.

Nico gives me a quick glance. "I like to drive. You might want to buckle up."

I slip on the seatbelt and take a deep breath.

"Are you ready?" he asks.

I nod. The car takes off, flying down the road, and I scream. I had no idea cars could go this fast. Nico lets out a whoop, and the gorgeous machine goes even faster. The engine is so much louder than the one in Ryne's black car. It vibrates to the point that I can feel it in my bones.

I let out a nervous laugh. This is the first time I've seen Nico smile since Nova died. We arrive in town faster than I even thought was possible, and Nico slows the car down.

"Fun, huh?" There's something about him that is so entirely different from his father, and I realize I've been tense around him for reasons that aren't his fault. Maybe he's nothing like Anders.

"A little. It was scary." I offer him a genuine smile.

"You'll get used to it."

He pulls up in front of a bright blue house right on the water. "Where are we?" I ask.

"My house."

I deflate. Looks like I'll be eating with his house-keeper. At least he doesn't live with Anders anymore. Since they buried Nova on Anders's property at the family graveyard, I wondered if that meant he still lived there.

"We won't stay long, but I want to introduce you to Mattie, my housekeeper. Then we'll join all the others for dinner at Ryne's house."

I blink at him because none of what he said makes

an ounce of sense. "Why do you want to introduce me to Mattie?"

He bites his bottom lip. "Well, I've had a difficult time since Nova died, but I'm obligated to choose a wife. Nova confided in me your fears of being sent to the mating house and of my father. She told me that you deserved better and made me promise to help you if I could." He clears his throat. "So that's why I've chosen you to be my wife. We'll have to keep up appearances of course, and we can't tell anyone." He takes both of my hands in his. "I don't expect this to be a marriage of love at all. Maybe eventually, but it will be a deep friendship. I hope that is acceptable to you."

When I don't say anything, he smiles conspiratorially. Then he jumps out of the car and comes around to open my door. I sit there in stunned silence, and he squats next to me. "You okay? You look a little pale."

I blink at him. "Did you just propose to me?"

He chuckles and runs a hand through his hair. "I guess so, yeah. Well, what do you say? Be my wife?"

CHAPTER 14

"I DON'T EVEN KNOW *what* to say," I sputter. "Are you allowed to ask me this early? Don't you have to wait until the Harvest Moon Festival?"

He grimaces. "I take it, that's a no?"

Is it? I would be stupid to say no. This is exactly what I've been wanting. Nico would be perfect. He is looking for a friendship and someone to give him space to grieve his true mate. Marrying him would keep me out of so many dangerous situations that could ruin my life.

Ryne's face pops into my head.

Ryne—who wants to marry Elle.

This is not what my heart has longed for, but he is my best option. Justin's face flashes in my mind. He would be a good mate as well, but there's no guarantee he'll choose me. Nico could still change his mind by the fall, but if he doesn't, this could be what I've been waiting for.

"It's a yes," I say at last.

"Good." He hugs me awkwardly. We don't kiss, thank goodness.

He takes me inside the beautiful home and explains that we can't tell anyone we're secretly engaged because it might put a target on my head. I have to agree with him there, but I don't tell him why. I'm not sure I'm ready to open up to him about my sad little investigation, not to mention the fact that Ryne asked me to keep things quiet. If Nico knew what I knew, he'd go mad trying to find Nova's killer. It might be better for him not to know.

But Ryne has been ignoring me for ages, spending all his free time dating Elle, and I'm growing tired of nursing my broken heart.

Maybe I should confide in Nico after all.

We go from room to room of his home, and he shows me his library and music room. He avoids the master bedroom. I wonder if he and Nova slept in the same bed together. I suspect they did. She loved him. They were fated and going to get married.

We head down to the kitchen, where a stout woman stands at the counter, her hands covered in flour. "What do we have here?" the woman asks.

"This is Poppy. She was a friend of Nova's. Poppy, meet Mattie."

She grabs a towel and wipes off her hands, but instead of shaking my hand, she wraps me in a tight embrace and whispers in my ear. "Any friend of Nova's is a friend of mine."

She lets me go, and tears glisten in her eyes. She wipes them with the back of her hands. "Goodness me, I'm sorry. I didn't mean to go all weepy."

Nico reaches over and squeezes her hand. "We all miss her."

Mattie clears her throat and busies herself with whatever it is she is making. "Tell me about yourself, Poppy. Where are you from?"

"Northwest. My village grew and harvested the cotton."

"Ah, nice. So you like to work outside."

"Very much so." I can't help but smile at the memories. If only I could relive them, I'd be so grateful for all of it, even the hardest days.

"What of your family?"

It's odd. She's the first person to ask me about my family since I've arrived. A twinge of homesickness pricks my heart. "My mother and father are good people. I have a little brother and a twin sister." My voice catches at the mention of Willow.

"Twins, huh? I bet that was fun. So you were born first?"

I shake my head. "No. She died."

Mattie's smile falls, and her eyes fill with sympathy. "I'm sorry, my dear. Were you close?"

I drop my eyes. "She was my best friend."

Silence fills the room, and I blink back my own tears.

Nico rests his hand on my back. "We have to go. Dinner will be starting soon, and no one wants to be late for one of Ryne's dinners."

Dinner is an awkward and uncomfortable affair. A long table with white cloth has been set up in Ryne's beautiful backyard. The swimming pool reflects the moonlight in the background. It's the first time I've seen one up close, and the clear water sparkles under the stars.

We're at the end of the table, and Anders sits next to Nico, speaking too loudly the entire time and monopolizing the conversation. And his date, Faye, laughs at all his inappropriate jokes. I sit quietly through it all and pick at my food, trying and failing to avoid looking at the couple directly across from me-- Ryne and Elle.

I hate that they're eating with us, but I'm also secretly happy to have Ryne so close. I could reach out and touch him if things were different. When Anders and Faye leave immediately following dessert, everyone nearby seems to be grateful. We finish up, and the other couples start to clear out. I keep waiting for Nico to suggest we leave as well, but he doesn't seem to be in any hurry.

Before I know it, it's the two of us with Elle and Ryne. And it hurts, because last time I was in this house, Ryne held me close, telling me that he wanted to kiss me.

Now, he is with his unofficial fiancée, and I guess I am too.

"Let's have drinks in the living room, shall we," Elle offers. There's no denying the tension in the air, but she does an excellent job of smoothing things over.

"Of course." I fake a smile.

I've had a hard time keeping my eyes off of Ryne all night, and he glanced at me quite a bit too. I have no idea what it means, except that I know it's not fair to Elle and Nico. Whatever's going on between me and Ryne didn't end the day of the ice-skating date, even though it should have.

We travel into the warm house. Ryne and Elle both sit in armchairs, so Nico and I take the plush couch. He slings his arm casually around me, and Ryne narrows his eyes. I snuggle into Nico, not because I want to be close to him, but simply because I want to see Ryne's reaction.

I shouldn't do it—again, it's not fair—but I can't help myself. I notice how his hands clench at the armrests on his chair, and a vein pops up in his neck. I almost laugh. He has no claim on me, and yet the slightest attention from one of the betas, and he's ready to pounce.

Nico swirls his wine in his glass. "So, Ryne, I have a question for you."

Ryne tears his eyes away from me and glowers at Nico. "Yes?"

"Well, you gave me permission to marry Nova at the wolf moon, and Poppy and I have come to an agreement, so what do you say about letting me take her on the pink moon?"

Ryne's face turns pale, then red, and then purple. He jumps out of his seat.

"What is with this girl?" he asks, and no one responds. Ryne paces in front of us, clenching and unclenching his fists. He points at me with an accusing finger. "First, Anders asked me if he could take you on the wolf moon, and then Justin asked me a couple of weeks ago for permission to marry you earlier than the harvest, and now Nico. What sorcery is this? How have you bewitched all my men?" He locks eyes on me, and I meet them defiantly. I'm not scared of him.

I keep my seat next to Nico and lay a hand on his knee. "Nico is the first man to ask me properly. You know how I feel about Anders, and I thought Justin wanted to marry Faye. Justin certainly never said a word to me about marriage." I swallow and steal a glance at Nico. His face is a mask of indifference. So much for help from him. I straighten my shoulders. If marrying Nico gets me out of the possible clutches of Anders or a mating house, I'm not going to turn that down. "I like

Nico. He's a good man who will treat me right. I see no reason to wait."

Ryne jams his hands into his hair, his eyes wild. They land on Nico, sharp as an axe splitting wood. "No. Absolutely not. I only gave permission for Nova because she wasn't a claimed woman, and she was your fated mate. Poppy is neither of those things."

I raise a defiant eyebrow. "And how do you know I'm not Nico's fated as well?"

"Because he was fated to Nova, and no wolf has ever had more than one."

Elle clears her throat. "But what of Justin or Anders. Perhaps she is their fated?"

"She's not," Ryne snarls. "That's impossible."

Elle narrows her eyes but doesn't respond.

Ryne spins back and hovers over Nico. "It's already an anomaly that so many mates have been found this year. I don't expect any more. You're going to have to battle it out with the others for Poppy's hand when the harvest moon comes this autumn. What is that? Eight months?" He motions between us. "Whatever this is between you two, it can wait eight months. Now get out of my sight."

Ryne storms back to his chair and throws his weight into it. He picks up his glass from a side table and downs it with a shaking hand.

Nico stands and offers me his hand. "I think we've overstayed our welcome."

"No, not Poppy," he growls. He doesn't look up, and a sheath of black hair covers his face. "She'll go back to the house with Elle. I don't trust you alone with her tonight." He grumbles into his drink, "Or ever."

Nico looks like he wants to argue, but he doesn't. Instead he leans down and places a gentle kiss on my cheek and squeezes both of my hands with his. "I can wait eight months, but you'll have to keep working hard to stay out of the bottom two positions on the board."

I don't like that. He doesn't either. It would be so much easier to just get married now. But that's not what I want. Deep down, Nico is a consolation prize. Which is fine considering I'm the same thing to him.

"Goodnight, Nico."

"And don't you dare announce your intentions to anyone," Ryne says as Nico makes for the door. "You will both continue with the claiming as normal."

As if any of this is normal.

Nico glares invisible daggers at Ryne and leaves.

Ryne won't meet my eyes, but I can't look away. It's as if I'm daring him to look at me. Somehow, I know that if he does, he won't be able to hide the truth any longer.

Elle must sense it. She's no fool. The second we're alone, she drops her pleasantries, striding into the middle of the living room, hands on her hips and long braids swinging. "Ryne," she snaps, "tell me the truth right now, or so help me, I will leave the Carolina Pack and never look back."

He has the audacity to try to look confused, but he doesn't say anything.

"Tell me." Her tone goes dry. "Just tell me."

He shakes his head once and takes another drink.

I'm riveted, watching this whole thing unfold, glued to the couch but wanting to interrupt. I have enough common sense to keep my mouth shut. I've never been able to get Ryne to admit his true feelings for me, nor the reason behind those feelings, but I'm also not Elle.

Elle is a force of nature, a luna with confidence and power radiating from her every pore. She's not someone to be messed with, and I don't think he could lie to her even if he wanted to. He said that wolves can't lie to each other about fated mates, which is exactly what I suspect we are. And what I'm pretty sure Elle suspects as well.

She lunges for me, and I scramble back onto my couch. Part of her begins to shift, her teeth elongating, her eyes changing shape. She snarls savagely, like she's going to kill me!

Ryne is there in seconds, ripping her away and tossing her across the room. He turns on her and growls, prepared to defend me. His wolf is practically bursting to the surface.

And just like that, she's back to herself, part of her silk dress shredded. "I knew it!" She gasps. "She's your fated mate!"

Ryne has nothing to say, but he doesn't shake his head.

"She has to be," Elle continues. "There's no way you'd defend her over me if she wasn't."

This is it. Finally. Ryne's been caught, and now that the truth is out there, he'll have to accept me. "You're right," he says at last. The words rip through him as if they cause him physical pain. I sink farther into the couch.

"But I wish she weren't."

The adrenaline racing through my veins turns to ice and my heart breaks.

Elle holds his gaze. "And why's that? She's beautiful, and you obviously like her. Don't forget that I caught you guys making out."

"I can't help my attraction to her, but she's not you," he says. "I made a promise to you, Elle. And I intend to keep it."

And at that, my heart doesn't just break--it shatters.

CHAPTER 15

"THAT MAN, I swear. I thought his father was stubborn," Elle says. We're in the car heading home. Ryne didn't utter another word to us after he said he was still going to marry Elle even though we are fated.

I don't even know how to respond. Part of me is still in shock, I think.

Knox meets my eyes in the rearview mirror. They are laced with concern. He wasn't present for the confession in the living room, but he had to have felt our energy the second we got into the car. Elle hasn't said aloud that Ryne and I are fated, but if she keeps going, she's bound to let it slip. What does he think is going on? More than that, what would he do if he knew I was fated to Ryne? Would he forgive me? Would he help me?

"We'll figure this out," Elle says, patting my leg.

"There's nothing to figure out," I choke on the

words. What's done is done. If Ryne doesn't want me, then I don't want him.

Period.

Her mouth drops open in surprise. "What on earth do you mean? Of course there is. I will not stand between you. That will not end well, no matter what Ryne said back there."

I peer out the window into the darkness. I don't want to look at Elle or Knox right now. I don't even want to be having this conversation.

"I'm serious," Elle goes on. "There's got to be a way to make this work."

I let out a laugh. "What about all that stuff you said before, about needing the marriage to bring your families together or whatever?" I don't know why I'm not fighting for him at this point. Yes, I do. It's because he rejected me. Who wants to fight for someone that doesn't want you? Not me. That's for sure.

Except... I do.

I want him with my whole soul. Something about hearing him say the words changed everything. He is *my* fated. I belong with him, and he belongs to me. How could he not want me? His actions have harmed me worse than he could ever know, and I doubt I'll ever get over it.

"Knox," she says, catching me off guard. "Can you stop the car, please? Poppy and I need to continue this conversation in private."

Knox does exactly as she says, his face stony as he leaves the car.

Elle turns on me. "Listen, Poppy. None of that stuff with our parents matters now. Those things have a way of sorting themselves out when fated mates come into the picture. We'll get Thorn to understand, and my parents too."

I snort. She's losing her mind if she thinks that will go over smoothly. Who am I to them? Nothing but a stupid human girl. And Elle is a powerful luna. Together Elle and Ryne could change the course of history. They're perfect for each other.

"If I found my fated mate, I wouldn't be denying him," she says softly, "and Ryne would totally support me in that. He's been my friend for years. I can't deny him his happiness." She crosses her arms. "Don't you want to be with him?"

"Of course I do, but you heard him. He doesn't want to be with me." I try to keep the pain out of my voice.

She gives a short laugh. "That is so not true. I've suspected this for a while now. I see how he watches you. He's denying it over some sense of stupid duty. I need to talk to Madame Delphine. She'll see reason, and if anyone can convince him, it's going to be her."

I'm pretty sure Madame Delphine already knows, so Elle's little plan is useless, but I grip her arm anyway, just in case I'm wrong. "You can't tell her. You can't tell anyone."

She gapes at me. "Why the hell not?"

"Because Ryne wouldn't want you to. He obviously wants to keep this a secret, or he would've told her himself. Look, if he doesn't want me, Nico is my best option. I don't want to mess that up."

"Nico won't care."

"Yes, he will! He won't want me if he knows I'm meant for his alpha. Think about it. That's dangerous territory."

"So, what? We go on pretending?"

I nod and slink back into the seat.

She rolls her eyes. "Oh yes, I can see us all a few years from now. Both Nico and I are trapped in loveless marriages, while you and Ryne screw on the side. No thank you. Nico might not care, but I do."

I flinch away from her. I would never . . .

Maybe I don't know what I would or wouldn't do. If Ryne were to come to me even after I was married, I'm not sure I'd be able to resist him. My face burns at the thought of being a woman like that. And I'd never want to hurt Nico. Would it hurt Nico though? He doesn't want to be physical with me; he needs a wife who will leave him alone. But it would hurt Elle.

"I think you're missing your chance at happiness," Elle says. There's something in her voice that she's not telling me. I study her for a minute. I can't believe I didn't see it before.

"You don't actually want to marry Ryne, do you?"

Her face stills, and the answer is obvious. She's hoping we get together so she can have an out.

She throws the door open without answering and orders Knox back into position.

The rest of the drive is silent until the car stops in front of the manor. Knox's eyes catch mine again, and this time they're pleading, but he doesn't say anything. I wish we could talk about this. By now he's figured out the truth about my relationship with Ryne. In another life, it would have been the two of us together, but in this one, he's going to be forced to serve the man who's fated to his first love. If only I could help him get out of here, or maybe find a love of his own. But that's impossible.

So many unsaid words pass between us until he breaks our gaze.

He gets out of the car and opens our door. Elle climbs out first, still huffing, and I follow. Knox meets my eye. "I'm so sorry," he mouths to me. I nod because I don't know what else to say.

At least he doesn't hate me.

I follow Elle into the house, and she turns to me in the entryway. "I'll keep this quiet for now, but only because you asked me to. After I think this through, I might tell Delphine anyway."

"She can't make her son do anything." The only person who can do that is the alpha king, and he'd rage if his son defied him.

"Well, I have to think of what is best for me and my family. You understand, right?"

I nod, even though I'm not sure I do. I thought the best thing for her family was to marry Ryne. If this ends up in a war between her father and Thorn, there's no telling what could happen.

But I'm just a dumb claimed girl.

What do I know?

***

Nothing changes.

Days pass in endless monotony. The truth is out there, but Elle and Ryne continue on as if nothing happened. Neither of them is even talking to me anymore. It's as if I no longer exist. I get placed with Cade during weapons training even though I try getting in with Elle's group. Ryne thinks I need to learn the other weapons first. I don't want to be with Cade. I'm ninety percent certain he's a murderer, but out of respect for Abi, I can't say anything. I'm not too worried about him killing anyone else in our group--since he has no motive, but I don't want to go on a date with him.

At meals, Elle sits with the other groups now, forging bonds with them that feel like little knives in my back. I even tried to corner Ryne when I found him alone during one of my morning runs, but he shifted and took off into the forest before I could get a word out.

I know he saw me.

At first I was angry, but now I realize they've decided it's best to forget about me entirely, and I refuse to let them see my anger. I also refuse to be sad. Instead, I grow bitter. I shouldn't be surprised by their actions, but I am. Elle must have come to her senses about outing the situation, and Ryne is stubborn as a mule. What a match.

There's a full moon tonight, and we're only another moon cycle away from the next festival, so everyone is extra antsy in the house. Me more so than the rest of the girls because tonight is my first one-on-one date with Anders. That day he canceled and Abi and I planted the poppies instead was one of the happiest days I've had since coming here, but I guess this date had to happen eventually.

"Let me fix your hair and makeup," Joanna offers, her voice pitying. I frown at that.

"And I can pick out your outfit," Abi adds.

I'm grateful for my friends, and I know they're worried about my bitter attitude lately, but I shake my head. "I don't want to look good for Anders. He's already going to try something, so the last thing I need is to look good because he'll probably blame whatever happens on me. I just know it."

Abi's eyes widen. "He can't. He'll get exiled if he takes your innocence."

I snort at that silly word. From my trip to the mating

house, I know the wolves couldn't care less about innocence.

"You mean virginity?" I question. She goes pale, and Joanna laughs. "Do you really think he would be exiled? He's the head of the betas. Trust me, Anders has gotten away with worse." My mind flashes to images of Willow's severed body, her blood seeping into the September soil, and I don't say anything more.

I run a brush through my hair only once, skip the makeup entirely, and dress in my most unflattering gown. It's a bulky cut and lime green, casting my skin in a sickly complexion. The whole thing rustles like dead leaves when I walk.

I grin to myself. Perfect.

CHAPTER 16

ANDERS TAKES a tight grip on my arm as we make our way down the steps and out to the ferry boat. I've decided I hate going anywhere by boat and much prefer a car, but the shifters seem to love the old-world quality of these damned boats. I sigh and climb aboard. At least we're not alone. It seems we're going on a group date today because everyone else climbs in after us.

Anders settles beside me and leans down, whispering hot breath into my ear. "You think I don't know what you're doing? No makeup and an ugly dress? It's going to take far more than that to dissuade my affections for you. In fact, knowing how desperately you want me away from you, makes me want you even more."

I try to pull away, but he tugs me closer and wraps his arm around my waist, his fingers digging into my hips. Since it's the full moon tonight, we're doing our dates in broad daylight. Madame Delphine made all the betas promise to have us back before dusk.

The boat rocks gently as Anders leads us to the back, far from the driver. Everyone else takes seats up front. We're practically alone, which makes me panic a little, but I hope that he has the decency not to try anything too awful right now. I also hope that he's not taking me back to his estate where he could get away with anything. But he can't, right? We're going on a date somewhere with everyone. And then he's bringing me back to the manor.

Maybe.

What would I do if he took me back to his estate? Would I fight or just let him have his way with me? I know if I fight, he'll kill me. But I don't know if I could bring myself to let him have me. My thoughts race to Ryne, wishing he would have the guts to accept me as his mate. Or at least keep me away from Anders. But Ryne has abandoned me.

Anders squeezes me up against his side, and I stare out over the water so I don't have to look at him. I try not to think about his disgusting body pressed against mine. He brings his face to my neck and kisses me along my hairline. I feel his hot breath under my hair and squirm. He laughs at that and kisses my jaw. Another woman might find him attractive, but I know better. Every cell in my body is screaming at me to run, but where would I go? He yanks me to him and presses his lips against mine. I keep my mouth closed and try not to cry.

This date will not end well.

Think of something else, anything else. My mind lands on the book Justin's mom gave me, and I start to recall the names of all the roses. I want to check on the poppies tomorrow. And maybe I can start growing some other plants in the greenhouse. What about irises? I wonder if Shauna could help me with those. And I'm sure the vegetable garden will need to be planted soon too. Maybe I can request it as part of my daily chores.

Anders's lips part, and I expect to feel his slimy tongue, but instead he moves back to my neck, and his teeth graze the skin. He bites down hard, and I yelp, jumping away from him. He tightens his grip on me and bites down even harder. Tears fall unbidden from my eyes, and I cry out again. I thought I was with a wolf, not a vampire. Granted, all paranormals, except for the shifters and lycans, died during the wars, but Anders would've made an excellent vampire. He's so cold and awful. Mercifully, he pulls away. I bring my hand up to my neck, expecting to find blood, but I don't.

"Good," he growls. "That will bruise nicely. Now everyone will know you're mine."

I want to protest. To tell him that I'll never be his. But I know that will only provoke him. Instead, I keep my face turned down and wipe away the tears.

He grips my chin with his free hand and forces me to

look at him. His dark eyes bore into mine. There's nothing there but hate and anger. "Oh, poor Poppy, did that hurt?"

I don't give him the satisfaction of an answer.

He smashes his lips against mine again. I try to keep them shut, but he forces them open with his tongue. He shoves his long tongue into my mouth, and I gag, wiggling to get away from him. He doesn't let go.

Once again, I let myself get lost in the thoughts of the different kinds of roses—the Bonica is a light pink rose that smells amazing, the Falstaff is a huge dark red rose, the French Lace is a pretty white one . . . Rose after rose comes unbidden to my mind as Anders continues to assault my mouth.

The boat shudders against a dock, and he pulls away. My mouth feels bruised and my lips sore. Anders gives me a wicked grin. "Perhaps after the show, we'll retire to my home for a few hours. As you will be my wife, I see no reason to wait until after the harvest festival."

I don't think there are enough roses in that book for a few hours at Anders's house. I'll never agree to go with him. I'd rather die.

He leads me along a cobblestone street, and the other couples join us. Everyone is walking the same direction, and there's a general sense of excitement among the crowd. I wish my friends were here. Since there's only five betas, the other girls today aren't the type to look out for me. Maybe Anders really will try to take me back to his place.

"Where are we going?" I ask, my voice cracking.

"The Manhattan Pack has a traveling show. They are excellent performers. I never miss them when they come into town."

"Seems like everyone else enjoys them as well," I say, pointing to the other couples.

"It is a treat," he says. "You're lucky I picked you for this date, Poppy. But then again, you should get used to it. I expect my wife to be submissive and agreeable, and in return, I will lavish her with the finer things in life."

I try not to sneer at that.

The line is long once we reach the theater. I expect Anders to cut to the front, but he doesn't. Though perhaps that is because those in line are other betas and their wives. A woman walks through the crowd with a basket of flowers. She stops at each couple and puts a flower in the woman's hair and another in the lapel of the man's coat. She reaches us. "What would you like?" she asks.

I spot a poppy among the flowers and point. She grins at me, offers a knowing nod, and tucks it behind my ear.

"And you?" she asks Anders. Her smile turns fake.

He selects a yellow rose, which I recognize as a Landora.

She tucks it into his lapel and moves on.

We enter the theater, and an usher leads us up to a box with an excellent view. Moments after we sit down, Nico and Faye join us. I meet Nico's eyes, pleading with him to rescue me, but he only gives me a stiff nod.

Are we still engaged? Were we ever?

Apparently Anders thinks we're engaged, and he never even asked me. I glare at him when he's not looking, hating everything about him. I don't care that he's conventionally attractive, that he has a high title, that he's strong and wealthy. He's a bad man, and he deserves to pay for all the women he's hurt.

Grady sits down next to Bailey, and he gives me a little frown, his eyes darting to the bruise on my neck. I shake my head, and he looks away, but I can tell by the set of his jaw that he's angry. I wish Joanna were here. It's stupid that she doesn't get to come on all the dates with him, even though everyone thinks she should. What's the point otherwise? But Bailey is a nice and quiet girl, so she's perfect for something like this. Her eyes twinkle with excitement, gazing out toward the curtain. I'm happy for her.

"Pathetic," Anders grumbles, glaring right at the poor girl.

My courage sparks. "What's pathetic?" Because I can think of someone, and he's sitting right next to me.

"Bailey ought to be sent to a mating house." Anders turns on me with a low voice. "She's clearly not attractive, nor athletic, but because she's smart, she keeps her name up on the leaderboard."

I snort. "Didn't know you cared so much, Anders."

"Of course I care. All beta men care about their wives." Anders shifts a little in his seat. I can't forget that he's had several wives over the years. "And as the top beta, who my men marry is of great importance to me."

"Well, I don't think Grady minds this date," I snap back. "And Bailey is a catch."

His nostrils flare as if he smells something rancid. "Do you remember what I said the first day I met you? We want subservient and submissive. We want refined and elegant." His eyes travel down my body, as if he can see right through my ugly dress. "We want sexy and strong."

I glare because how could I not remember the first time I met this devil?

"Bailey is none of those things. But maybe you're right, and Grady doesn't mind, considering he's so infatuated with that loud-mouthed Joanna." He grimaces. "If you ask me, she's the least desirable woman in the house. Betas should have strong wives to create strong bloodlines. Ryne should've sent her off to the mating house ages ago."

"Well, nobody asked you," I spit. I want to go on, to argue that Joanna is literally the best, but the lights flicker and dim.

Just before the show begins, Ryne and Elle slip into

the back of the box. I spin, and Ryne's gaze lands on the bite mark on my neck. His eyes go dark, but before he says anything, the lights in the theater go off, and the stage lights up.

CHAPTER 17

THE NEXT HOUR is filled with singing and dancing—a wonderful story unfolding between talented actors, unlike anything I've seen before. It's a kind of magic that I didn't even know existed. Everything fades into the background as I watch the stage with rapt attention. The show is a reenactment of the common fairy tale known as "Little Red Riding Hood," but in this case, the wolf is a real shifter. He shifts between man and wolf and has a love story with the girl, but she doesn't know about his wolf side. The huntsman is the girl's other love interest, who actually turns out to be the villain. The poor wolf shifter is so misunderstood, so afraid to tell Red the truth of his identity.

Just as things are getting good, the lights lift.

"What?" I squawk. "It's over?"

Anders chuckles. His arm is on the back of my chair,

and he curls it around my shoulders, pulling me in. "This is only a little intermission. Don't worry. In ten minutes they'll start the rest of the show."

"Oh, good." My voice trails off when I notice his ice blue eyes staring at the mark he inflicted on my neck like it's his own personal brand.

"I have to go to the bathroom." I jump up and run out of the theater box. I don't really have to go, but ten minutes away from Anders is just what I need right now.

The second I step outside, however, I think leaving was a mistake.

The lobby is filled with large shifter men and their stylish wives, and there are far more men than women. They're not all married, I know that. I also know I'm not safe here. Not with men like these. The crowd thickens, and I catch Anders among them. He's looking for me. My heart rate speeds as I duck into the crowd, dodging bodies as I go. I bump into a few people who shoot me scathing looks. My cheeks prickle, but I don't stop to apologize. I need to get out of here. I don't want him to show me off to these people... or worse. I spot a dark hallway and hurry inside. Hopefully I can hide out here until the intermission is over. It's empty in here and cold and perfect. I lean against the wall, closing my eyes and catching my breath.

Someone grabs my arm, and I jump. "Hey!" My training kicks in, and I jerk away, readying my stance.

"It's only me." Ryne looms over me. His eyes flick to

the poppy behind my ear, and his gaze softens for a brief moment. That one look sends my mind reeling. I'm angry. I'm thrilled. I don't know what I am.

"You've been avoiding me." I say the thing I've wanted to say for what feels like forever. "Why?"

He stares at me for a long moment, and I think maybe he won't answer me at all. "Because I want to keep you safe," he whispers at last. And then he glares at me, but it's not as though any of this is my problem.

I roll my eyes, fed up with his games. "How is avoiding me keeping me safe?"

He shakes his head. "You don't understand anything."

"So enlighten me."

He pauses for a second, his stormy gaze lingering on my lips before traveling over to my neck. "Did Anders do that?" His jaw pops.

I ball my hands into fists. He suddenly cares? He doesn't get to have it both ways.

"I said, did Anders do that?" His words are clipped, eyes glued to the bite mark.

"What do you think?" I spit out. "Of course he did. And he has big plans to take me back to his house tonight too."

"The hell he does." Ryne slams his fist into the plaster, bits of it breaking and falling to the ground.

And then he's gone.

I'm back to being angry. I can never get what I want

from this man. Maybe I never will. Tears well in my eyes, and I wipe them away and gather myself. Now that my nerves have had a chance to calm down, I realize I'm foolish to be hiding out back here. What if it hadn't been Ryne who found me?

So I leave and wander around the lobby for the rest of the intermission, weaving through the crowds, catching bits and pieces of people's conversations. Most of it means nothing to me. A lot of the people here keep staring at me, but I try to ignore them. A few women seem interested in the poppy. Maybe it's unfashionable and childish to have a flower tucked behind my ear, but I don't care. I've recently decided they're my favorite flower.

The lights flash, and I head back to the box. I'm excited to see what happens to Red and the wolf, but I'm not excited to spend more time with Anders or to face Ryne and Elle. I find my seat, and Anders is waiting for me with a suave smile and a bag of buttery popcorn. I haven't had popcorn in ages. It was a special treat we made only on special occasions back home. I liked it okay, but it was Willow's favorite, so I take the bag and try to forget about her murderer at my side, imagining that I'm here with my sister instead. What would she have thought of all this? Would she have liked any of these betas? Would she have ended up in a mating house?

I don't know, but I'm certain she'd have fought tooth and nail to change things.

I want that to be me. I want to do something.

Nova's face flashes through my mind. After she died, I made a promise to myself that I would do something, but it's been two months, and I'm no closer to making a difference around here. I have to talk to Abi again and see if she'll finally let me go to Ryne with her suspicions about Cade. My biggest problem is that even though Cade had a motive to kill Lexi, he didn't with Nova. Unless it's like Abi said, and when he ditched her on the dance floor, it was to follow Nova. Seems unlikely. Maybe we've got nothing here. Maybe accusing Cade will only get us targeted. I don't know what to do.

The lights dim, and the show resumes. I'm not pulled into the story as quickly this time around. Instead, I study the men around me: Anders, Nico, Cade, Justin, Grady, and Ryne.

Unlike the twisted fairy tale playing out on stage, the one playing out in my life is much closer to the original story. One of these men is the Big Bad Wolf—now I need to figure out who.

Before I know it, the show is over. Despite my racing thoughts, I still found it a delightful experience. I hope that Nico and I are able to get married, and he'll bring me to the theater every time they are in town. I swallow hard. I don't much like thinking about marrying Nico because I want to be with Ryne, but he made it very clear that that'll never happen. After that weird little exchange we had in the hallway, he went right back to ignoring me.

I stand and stretch. Anders puts a hand on my back and leans in to whisper in my ear. "Tonight is the full moon. Let's go back to my house and lose track of time so you have to stay with me all night."

I throw up a little in my mouth, then crane my neck around and meet Ryne's eyes. He very much looks like he wants to kill Anders. Well, at least Ryne's paying attention to me again, and I would gladly step aside and let him tear Anders limb from limb.

Instead, he calls out to the betas. All five men turn to him. The power Ryne wields over them is incredible. It's as if they couldn't disobey him even if they wanted to. Maybe they can't.

I use the opportunity to take a couple of steps away from Anders and run right into Nico. He glances at my neck and gives me a strained smile. I reach over and squeeze his hand. I don't want him to think that I want anyone but him.

Ryne continues. "It's still a few hours from dusk, so I've arranged to send your dates back in the cars. We need to prepare for the lycans."

I expect Anders to protest, but he doesn't. Relief fills my chest. I wonder how often I can get away with this. At some point, I'll have a private date with him that I won't be able to get out of. There are roughly seven months until the next harvest. A lot can happen in seven months.

We leave the men in the box, and Elle leads us to the cars. One is Ryne's, and Knox opens the door for me. I climb in back and get stuck between Faye and Bailey. Elle rides up front. We start to drive, and I lean back into my seat, letting my eyes drift shut. Maybe I can finally relax. That's when Faye presses her pointy finger against the mark on my neck. I flinch.

"Ooooh, looky there. Somebody's been a naughty girl." She cackles, and Bailey averts her eyes.

I slap my hand over the stupid hickey as my cheeks redden. Maybe those women weren't looking at the poppy behind my ear after all. "You're one to talk," I mutter.

She stiffens. "No, I'm not. I don't do anything with any of the betas that I don't plan to marry. Justin's the only one I've kissed."

I want to say something about Thorn and Ryne—kissing father and son in one night—but I don't because that would be unnecessarily cruel. As much as I hate her, I don't want to sink to her level.

Instead, Elle rescues me. It's the first she's spoken to me in what feels like forever. "Did you know that Justin, Nico, and Anders have all asked Ryne for permission to marry Poppy early? Looks like you might need to set your sights on Cade instead. Though I do believe he's due for a private date with Poppy next, so that might not work either."

I flush and drop my eyes. I'm not sure if that made things better or worse. Either way, Faye doesn't say another word the rest of the way home. Her anger fills up the car with her silence, and I try to inch away from her. She's definitely not happy, and an unhappy Faye is the last thing anyone needs, least of all me.

<h1 style="text-align:center">CHAPTER 18</h1>

JOANNA IS STAYING with us tonight because Grady had to go protect the city from the lycans. She sets up a cot next to mine, and even though I hate the circumstances, I love having her back at my side. I have a long silver sword under my cot, and she has a bow and arrow. We're all armed, so if anyone tries anything tonight, they won't survive.

The full moon feels so different this time. We've been through months of these terrifying moons, but this is the first time we've actually been able to protect ourselves. Along with the sword tucked right under my cot, I have a pair of daggers under my pillow. If something comes for me, I'm not going down without a fight.

"Alright, girls," Madame Delphine says, "this is your last chance to use the restroom before we lock the door. Elle will accompany anyone who needs to go. Hurry, please. It's already starting to get dark, and the moon is rising as we speak."

Joanna widens her eyes. "Nature calls."

"I'll go too, just in case." I already went, but I drank a lot of water at dinner, and the last thing I need is to be stuck in that room with a full bladder. It used to be if someone really needed to go, she could get a chaperone, but now we're always locked in from dusk until dawn. Nobody's complained though, not after what we've witnessed.

Joanna and I stand in line to use the restroom, and Elle waits a few paces down the hallway.

Joanna goes in first, and then I do my own business. A couple of other girls were behind us. We wait with Elle, but she keeps looking at the rising moon from the little window in the hallway. "You guys head on back. I'll wait for the other two girls."

I loop my arm through Joanna's, and we head on down the stairs. We're almost to the door of the gym when Joanna stops suddenly. "What is it?" I ask, not wanting to get stuck out here.

Her hand flies to her neck, and her expression crumples. "My necklace, the one Grady gave me, it's gone."

"Maybe you left it up in the room or even in your cot? Come on, we can find it in the morning."

"No, I had it on in the bathroom. I remember looking at it in the mirror. It must've fallen off on our walk back down. It won't take long. I can't lose that necklace. It was his mother's."

Grady's parents are both dead—something he only talks to Joanna about.

The sky is fully dark now, and we can hear Elle and the other girls coming down right behind us.

"Joanna, no. We'll find it in the morning."

"I can't lose that necklace." Her voice is adamant. There's no reasoning with her when she's like this.

She shakes out of my grip and turns back to the stairs. I follow, studying the floor. A howl pierces the air, and goosebumps rise on my skin. That one sounded like a lycan, but I can't be sure. Howls freak me out no matter what.

I rush for Joanna as Elle and the other girls meet up with her. We're all standing on the steps, Elle towering over us. "Joanna, we can't be out here," Elle hisses. Her eyes are wide, and I can sense her wolf is close at hand. She could shift at any moment.

Katelyn and Alyssa rush past us and down the steps.

"It'll only take me a second," Joanna insists. "The necklace had to have fallen off between here and the bathroom."

The moon still hasn't risen above the tree line, and all the lights in the house are turned off, so it's very dark. There's no way we'll find that necklace in time.

Elle grips Joanna's arm and pushes her back. I turn and head down the stairs.

"Let me go," Joanna says frantically.

"You're putting everyone at risk by being out here. Let's go."

A growl sounds from right behind them. Something else is on the stairs with us. To think that another monster got into this house, and so soon after the moon rising, makes me whimper. I can barely make out Elle's amber eyes in the darkness, but they go cold. "Poppy, you run. Joanna, you go with her." Her determined voice lends me strength. "I'll stay and fight the lycan. Lock the door. Don't worry about me."

"What? No way. We'll stay and help," Joanna says, her words cutting off with a scream. I can barely see what's happening but manage to catch Elle shift into her silver wolf as Joanna goes down hard, a dark monster on her back.

I grab for her hand to pull her away, ignoring the growls from the huge wolf-like animal. It's so dark I can't really make out its features, but at least Elle's silver wolf is easier to see. She lunges for it, and the creature shifts off Joanna to snap at Elle. She jumps back before its jaws can close around her neck. Then it goes for her neck again, and I'm sure it's going to succeed this time. I should run, but I can't leave her like this. I take advantage of its distraction with Elle and stomp on its foot. It howls and barely misses Elle. It's enough to give her the upper hand.

"We gotta go," I cry, grabbing Joanna by the arm and

dragging her toward the gym door, but she hangs equally as tight onto me, pulling me in the other direction.

"What are you doing?" I gasp.

"Trust me," she says.

The fight has moved up the stairs, so that's the last place we should go. But Joanna is determined. Against my better judgment, I follow her up the creaky steps, through the entryway, and out the front door. The cool March air hits me like a wall, and my heart slams against my ribcage.

Again, I ask her what she's doing.

"Remember when I said that the best time to run away from this place is during a full moon?" Her voice rises in excitement. "The wolves are distracted. Let's go now."

"What about that lycan that just attacked us in the house?" Or the fact that this entire area has patrols everywhere.

Joanna shakes her head. "That wasn't a lycan. That was a wolf." Her voice darkens as she says it, and goosebumps crawl across my skin. "I don't know why a wolf is targeting us girls, but it's more reason to get you out of here."

"Me? Aren't you coming too?"

She doesn't answer me. We stumble down the front steps and out into the yard. It's dead quiet, but in the distance, wolves continue to howl. Joanna hugs me and whispers low in my ear, so low that I can barely hear her.

"I never lost my necklace. That was a lie to give us more time."

"You planned this?"

"Yes. And I'm sorry, but I can't leave Grady. I thought I could, but I can't do it. So I'm helping you get out of here, and then I'll come back and say that a lycan took you. All we have to do is make it to the river where the two willow trees hang out across the bank. There's a boat and someone to take you to safety waiting there. But we have to hurry."

For a second, I entertain the idea. A few months ago, I would've taken her up on it. But now I know better. Frankly, I know too much.

I wrench away from her. Running away will set off a terrible chain of events, and that's if I don't die first. And if by some miracle I make it out of here alive and go to live in this unknown place that Joanna thinks will be a safe haven, the wolves might not believe Joanna. And if they don't believe that a lycan took me, if anyone can prove that I ran away, then my family will be slaughtered.

I don't want my fate to be a warning to others. I want my fate to be what saves us all.

"No," I whisper back. "There are a lot of things I'm willing to risk, but my family isn't one of them. And besides that, I want to help the Resistance here." I can barely see her in the darkness, but the rising full moon shines across her eyes, making them sparkle. "Get me in with them *here*. Let me help *here*."

She frowns. "But I wanted to save you."

"You can't." And then I turn back to the house.

Joanna groans with frustration but follows me back. When I step inside the manor, it's even quieter than it was outside. My mind races to Elle and that wolf who attacked Joanna. Did she catch him? Stop him? Where are they now?

We tiptoe through the entryway. Part of me desperately wants to turn on a light, but I know that will alert anyone lurking about to our presence. Maybe it's safer in the dark.

"We should've brought our weapons with us," I whisper.

Joanna slips a pair of daggers from the pocket of her pajama pants. Moonlight streams in through the windows, and the daggers glint silver. "You think I wouldn't have come prepared?"

She hands me one as we step farther into the darkness.

I hold the dagger in my right hand like it's my salvation. Maybe it is. We walk as quietly and quickly as we can. Once we reach the stairs, we head down, wincing every time one of them squeaks. We reach the landing to the basement, and it's darker than ever. I step forward and nearly trip over something soft.

"Ouch," Elle's soft voice moans out. She's in her human form, naked and in pain.

We kneel down. "Are you okay?"

"Yes." But she's curled in on herself, so she's obviously not. She's holding her hands against her stomach. Something dark and sticky pools by her side.

Blood.

"You don't look okay," Joanna says.

"I'll heal fast," Elle whispers back. "Go to the gym and knock so they can let you in."

"What happened to the other guy?" I ask.

As if on cue, a low growl rumbles from the top of the stairs.

CHAPTER 19

"GO!" Elle gasps. But I'm not leaving her here. Joanna and I pick her up and drag her toward the gym door.

"Open up!" I scream. "It's us!"

There's a scrape of metal, and a draft of cool air as the door opens. The growl turns into a snarl, and something flies toward us. We push Elle into the room, and I manage to make it in, but the wolf is back, and its jaw has a hold of Joanna's leg. It's more determined than ever.

She cries out. I throw my dagger, aiming for the beast's heart, but it's still hard to see anything. I miss and hit what I think is its shoulder, but it's enough to get him to release Joanna. We get her the rest of the way inside, and Madame Delphine slams the door shut, wrenching the lock in place. Her face pales, but she doesn't say anything. "Were any of you bit?"

I shake my head and tell her I wasn't.

"I . . . I . . . don't think so," Joanna says. It's strange seeing her scared. She's usually so fearless. But she was bit, wasn't she? It had her leg. I'm suddenly reminded of Charlotte and wonder if Joanna had been infected, if I'd have the courage to do something about it.

The lights flip on before I can find my answer.

Someone hands Elle a blanket, and she nods, "I was, but that wasn't a lycan." I've never heard her sound so angry. "That was one of ours."

Nobody knows what to say to that, and the room grows silent, the tension thick and suffocating. Everyone is awake. Some are sitting up in their beds, others are standing. Weapons are in most of their hands. They were prepared to fight a lycan. Would they fight off one of their own betas if it came down to it?

"Well, he sure got me good." Joanna hisses, lifting up her pant leg.

Madame Delphine kneels down and begins to examine her injuries. "Looks like you got a few nasty scratches, but no actual bites. I'll get you cleaned up, and then we'll go to bed. Elle, we have extra provisions. You can sleep in here tonight."

Elle laughs bitterly. "As soon as I'm healed, I'm going back out there and hunting that asshole down."

"I'm sorry, but under no circumstances am I opening this door again until sunrise," Madame Delphine returns. "You're going to have to stay here."

Elle glares, but she knows she won't win this fight.

We crawl into our beds, and Abi stares at us like we've risen from the dead.

"Are you okay?" she asks.

"We are."

A tear runs down her face. "I thought I was going to lose you the same way I lost Lexi."

"It's okay. We're here." I grab her hand and give it a squeeze. The truth is, she almost did.

"Oh, you have got to be kidding me," Joanna groans.

"What is it?"

"Grady's necklace." Her voice is angry. "I had it in my pocket. It must have fallen out when I pulled out the daggers."

Under normal circumstances, I would laugh and tell her it was karma for the lies she told. But instead, I just tell her we'll go find it first thing in the morning.

None of us sleep that night.

As soon as dawn breaks, Madame Delphine wrenches the door open. I've already folded up my cot and blankets. So has Joanna.

We're out the door before anyone else. Joanna races in front of me, studying the ground as we climb up the stairs. We don't find anything in the manor, so we go outside, our eyes scanning the grass. I can't believe after all that, she's still worried about the necklace. But I guess if Ryne had given me a necklace, I'd want to find it too.

"Found it," she cries out and bends down to grab it.

I catch up with her, and a flash of yellow catches my eye under the azalea bush next to the house. I crouch down and wrap my fingers around a yellow flower. It's a Landora rose. The petals are still tightly folded into a bud, and some of them are damaged or missing. The same exact one that Anders was given last night at the play. But before I can process what it could mean, I spot Elle. Her hair is mussed, and she bears down on us, her eyes blazing.

She reaches us and slaps Joanna across the face. Joanna and I both recoil. This is not the Elle that I know.

"You could've gotten us all killed last night. Don't think I don't know that you ran off in the opposite direction than I told you to go. You're reckless and foolish. Next time, I'll leave you to fend for yourself."

She turns on me. "And you—maybe you should get a better friend."

My mouth falls open. "Joanna is the best friend in the world. You have no idea what you're talking about." If only I could confess that Joanna only took those risks to try to get me out of here. Joanna is safe with Grady. There's no reason for her to help me, but she does because she cares about me. Maybe even cares about me more than anyone else in the world.

Elle glares. Joanna glares. I glare. We're some trio.

"Do you think you can find that wolf who attacked us?" I ask, forcing myself to change the subject before Joanna and Elle end up in a fight. My fingers still clutch the rose, a thorn pressing into my palm.

Elle shakes her head, even angrier than before. "It's been too long. I've lost his scent. But he could've killed me. Or you. Or Joanna."

"Well, that's obvious," Joanna snaps. "But why?"

It's the question none of us have an answer to.

But we have to drop it and get ready for the day. Of course, I find myself totally distracted in all my morning classes. A lot of us are, so Madame Vivien doesn't single me out during our morning exercises. She's been pulling me out for vigorous workouts less and less, which I hope means she's stopped blaming me for Charlotte killing Lucille. The day after the full moon is always like this, anyway. But I'm not distracted because of the waning moon; I'm distracted because I figured out who killed Nova and Lexi. The Landora rose said it all. It's so obvious, glaring me right in the face this whole time.

And I know his next victim: Joanna.

She was his target last night.

I have the proof sitting in my pocket. I just don't know who to trust with the information. I want to tell Elle, but she disappeared before breakfast, and I haven't seen her again.

The person I really want to tell is Ryne, but he's not around either. When is he ever?

Right before lunch, Nico and Grady poke their heads into the classroom. Nico wiggles his finger at me to come to him, and I glance up at Madame Vivien for permission. She waves her hand. Joanna is already in Grady's arms. I know I can trust Nico, but part of me is worried that I could be wrong about him. It's not like I can confide in him in the middle of class with everyone staring at me, so I get up from my seat and go to him.

He takes my hand and pulls me into the hall. "We've come to take you ladies out for the day."

"Why?" I ask, confused. "We weren't supposed to have dates today."

"We have news, and we're taking you out to celebrate."

I swallow hard. Would they be celebrating if they knew what I knew?

Somehow, I don't think so.

I climb into the passenger seat of Nico's pretty red car and quickly buckle my seatbelt. He takes off, and I fly back into my seat, gripping the handle on the door. Nico laughs. I don't know that I've ever heard him laugh. It almost breaks through my undercurrent of fear.

"What's the news?" I ask.

He peels my hand away from the leather seat and weaves his fingers into mine. "Ryne has agreed to let me and Grady take you and Joanna as brides at the Pink Moon Festival."

All the blood drains from my face, and my head feels like it's a million pounds. "What? He was so against it before."

Nico smiles and shrugs. "He called the two of us into a meeting this morning and said he found a couple of betas to replace us so the rest of the girls still have a shot with a beta. Isn't this great news?"

I nod absently and fake a smile. I should be happy. Now I don't have to worry about Anders pulling a stunt with me like he did yesterday. I bet that's why Ryne is allowing this. He's protecting me, like he said. And it might even protect some of the girls who are still in the house by bringing them more betas.

I still don't understand how Ryne can let me be with another man though. We're fated.

I don't want to be with Nico, but he's my second best option.

Ryne is the first, but he's rejecting me.

I look away and blink back tears. When I've gathered my strength, I smile back at Nico and squeeze his hand. His curly chestnut hair looks golden in the sunlight. It blows in the wind of his open window, and his tanned features wrinkle when he smiles at me. I can do this. Nico will treat me kindly and we'll just avoid any interaction with Ryne and Elle. Somehow I doubt this is going to go over well with the other betas though.

What's Anders going to do when he learns that he can't have me?

Lunch is a lively affair. Joanna is thrilled with the news and is excited for me. Now she probably doesn't feel like she has to help me escape. This is a win for all of us.

The rose I found this morning is still in my pocket, and I keep waiting for the right moment to bring it up. I'm not going to be able to get in front of Ryne, so these guys are my best option. But I'm not sure how Nico will react to the news, so I wait until he excuses himself to use the restroom to confess my secret to Grady and Joanna.

We're in the middle of dessert when I pull out the Landora.

"What's that?" Joanna asks.

I let out a breath. "Yesterday at the play, the flower girl gave this to Anders."

Grady raises a curious eyebrow. "Why do you have it?"

I swallow hard and look around one last time to make sure Nico is still in the bathroom. "This morning after we got out, I found this on the ground outside. Elle said the attacker was a wolf, not a lycan. Anders must have lost it off his clothes outside the manor when he shifted. I think he's the one who's killing the girls. And he tried to kill Joanna."

Grady's jaw tenses, and he turns on Joanna. "You were attacked?"

"That's not the point," she hisses, eyes going round. "Would you listen to Poppy, please?"

He turns back to me. "What are you saying?"

"I'm saying that Anders is the one who killed Nova and Lexi."

"How do you know that?"

I quickly tell him the whole story of what happened the night before. "Anders is a violent and cruel man. He killed my sister. He obviously lost that rose during his attack on Joanna. Look, someone has been killing women, and it stands to reason it's Anders. He only wants the highest caliber for his betas. Anyone who he doesn't feel deserves to be a beta wife has to go, and if it's not by way of the mating house, then he'll take them out himself." I take a deep breath, my gaze landing on Grady. "He doesn't think Joanna is good enough for you. He told me that yesterday at the play. That's got to be why he attacked her."

Grady stands, his fists clenched. "I'm going to kill that son of a bitch."

Joanna puts her hand on his arm. "Calm down. We need to think through this. Poppy's evidence is pretty damning, but we can't just go running after Anders and accuse him of all this."

I'm surprised. She's usually the one jumping head-first into danger.

Grady jams a hand through his hair and points at Joanna. "How can you say that? Did you forget that he tried to kill you last night? I can take him. He'll be dead before dinner."

I help Joanna get Grady back into his seat. "Listen, we need to figure out why he would be doing this before accusing him, right? Do you think it's safe to tell Nico?"

They exchange a look. "The bond between father and son is strong, and alpha's rule all, but *nothing* beats the bond between a wolf and his fated."

That sentence alone is like a jab to the heart.

"We have to tell Ryne," Grady says. "If we go about this the right way, none of us will get in trouble, and Anders will still be dead."

Nico returns, and we go quiet. He collapses into his chair. "What did I miss?"

I'm not sure what to do--if I should go ahead and tell him, or if it's best to wait and let things play out. I feel terrible keeping this secret. Are they right that he'd choose avenging his mate over protecting his father? It feels dangerous either way.

So I make a decision, put my fake smile back on my face, and say, "Nothing much. Do you want some of this?" I point to the plate of chocolate cake. "It's delicious, but I'm stuffed."

Grady and Joanna don't say anything. They're taking my lead on this.

Nico chuckles and leans back into his seat, stretching his arms out. "I'll have it finished in no time. Don't you worry your pretty head about it."

He's so nice. He deserves more. And all I can hope is that I'm not making a huge mistake by keeping this from him.

CHAPTER 20

LAST NIGHT, after our double date, Grady pulled me aside and told me that he would take care of Anders. He asked me to keep Joanna safe and to not tell anyone.

I'm not convinced it's the best idea, and if I have the opportunity, I will explain everything to Ryne. But I'm not counting on that, so for now, I'll keep my mouth shut. I go about my morning exercise and chores with my head down, taking what enjoyment I can from the perfect spring weather. I can't stop thinking about Grady and Anders. I hope Grady is alright. There aren't any betas here today, so I have no idea what's going on.

I finish up and get dressed in one of the simple cotton dresses our closets were equipped with last week. Mine is deep navy blue, and I kind of hate myself for thinking that it looks like Ryne's eyes.

On my way into the classroom, I pass by the rankings. There should be twenty-two girls here, but there are only thirteen of us left. I'm currently ranked number six. Now I'm battling for the top, but with Nico's news, none of that will matter by the next full moon.

That's if Anders doesn't get to me first.

I slide into my seat next to Abi. She's chipper today with a grin on her face from ear to ear because we're starting a section on writing. She and Bailey are the most avid readers of the bunch here, even more so than Joanna, and to say they're excited would be an understatement.

"Do you understand what this means?" She squeezes my arm. "We'll be able to send communications to each other."

Joanna smirks from her other side and whispers. "And why would you want to do that?"

Abi goes bright red and checks to make sure nobody is listening to our conversation. "You know, in case we need to help someone." She swallows and then whispers low. "I heard—someone—talking about the Resistance. Do you know anything about it?"

Joanna sits back, her face a mask. "Nope. But you should be careful who you talk to about that stuff."

Joanna and Abi don't know that I already talked to Madame Delphine about it. Of course the house mother denied anything and left abruptly.

I'm not sure what to say here, and I almost tell them, when Madame Delphine herself strolls in and interrupts us. "Ladies, we have a real treat for you today. Ryne has arranged a dinner cruise in the harbor. He has a few exciting announcements to make. You must wear your best dresses and make sure you do your hair and makeup like you would for a festival. There will be no afternoon classes, so you will have sufficient time to get ready."

I try not to think about the announcements, even though my betrothal will likely be one of them. Our writing class flies by, and before I know it, Elle is taking the seat across from us at lunch. She pops a french fry into her mouth. "So, what do you think the announcement is?" she asks.

"You mean you don't know?" Joanna snorts. "You must know."

Elle shakes her head. "Why would I know?" She doesn't say it in a rude way like Faye would have. She seems genuinely confused. I like her, and I hate her. It's such a weird feeling.

"Because you're Ryne's bride-to-be," Joanna says.

Elle meets my eye for just a moment but doesn't say anything about Ryne and me. I should've told Joanna everything. She's my best friend, but I don't want to admit that we're fated, and he *still* rejected me. I'm not even sure I could get the words out.

They hurt too much.

Abi plops down next to Elle. "So what's Ryne going to tell us?"

Elle's mouth drops open. "I don't know why you

think I know. It's not like I live with the guy. I'm a house mother *here*. Plus, this is all wolf business. He only discusses those things with Anders and a council of betas."

Joanna narrows her eyes. "Why is Anders the second? If you ask me, it should be Grady."

Elle chuckles at that. "Grady is welcome to challenge Anders for the position. Good luck."

"If something happened to Ryne, then Anders is in charge?" Her lip curls.

"He's not automatically alpha. But yes, he would step up and take Ryne's place until a new alpha surfaces. The men have to fight it out."

"And who would take over if they both died?" I ask. I'm pretty sure it's Grady because of how close they are, but then again, there are a lot of betas, and I only know a handful. Sometimes pack hierarchy can be confusing. Anders and Ryne don't seem all that close, and yet Anders is the second in command.

Elle scoffs. "If they both died, it would be a bloodbath. There isn't a direct line to anyone because Ryne doesn't have an heir yet, and King Tremaine doesn't have any other sons."

I've often wondered if Ryne has brothers. Guess not.

"There's only the alpha and his second. If they both died at the same time, then all the betas would battle for the position of alpha. I don't know if you've noticed this, but Anders and Ryne don't go to the same battles or patrol the same areas at the same time. It's not in the pack's best interest to have them together too much."

So maybe Ryne shouldn't be coming around here to oversee the claiming as much as he has this year. I can't help but wonder if that has something to do with me. It must, right? I'm his fated mate. Not that he cares. I'm looking right at the reason he won't be with me, and she's gorgeous, as always. Elle's braided hair is tied back in a long white silk ribbon, and she's wearing a silky white dress to match. It contrasts perfectly with her ebony skin, and all I can think is she'll look amazing in a wedding dress.

I shake the image clear of my head. "What about you?" I ask.

"What about me?" Her eyebrows furrow.

"You're a wolf. Could you ever be an alpha?"

She drops her eyes and swallows. "No. I'm a female. Males aren't allowed to fight me, so I could never challenge an alpha for his role."

"But what if you did?" My tone is goading, but I don't care. I want to know. I shift forward in my seat and stare her down, willing her to answer me.

"The betas would detain me. They wouldn't let me fight," she says at last.

I lean back in my seat. "Well, that doesn't seem fair."

Joanna cracks a smile. "So you've thought about this? Hmm, Princess Elle has a nice ring to it, but it's not better than Alpha Elle."

She bristles and shushes us. "Keep your voices down."

"Okay, but answer us. You'd love to be alpha, wouldn't you? I can tell. It's in your blood."

She studies us, as if weighing whether she can trust us. "When I was a kid, I told my father I'd be the alpha one day, and after beating me for my insolence, he explained why that would never happen."

"He beat you?" Abi whispers. She's been watching this conversation unfold with round saucer eyes, her food completely untouched.

Elle lifts a shoulder and drops it. "It's not a big deal. I was a spitfire of a child, and he worried that I would cross Thorn. It hurt, but at least I'm still alive. If I had told Thorn that I wanted to be an alpha, he might have killed me on the spot." She takes time to look us each in the eyes. "And he still would. So when I tell you that I do not want to be the alpha, I mean it."

"This is a dangerous world to be born a woman in, isn't it?" Joanna asks, but it's not really a question. Nobody says anything more about it.

I push my chicken salad around my plate, no longer hungry. I wonder if that's why Ryne rejected me. If his father was that cruel, and he didn't want me to be Ryne's wife, then he'd probably kill me. I just wish I knew for sure. If Ryne would sit me down and explain everything, then maybe I could let him go. Maybe I wouldn't have to hurt so much.

"Come on, ladies, it's time to get ready. Joanna needs to pick our dresses," Elle says with a smile. She's acting casual, but her smile doesn't reach her eyes, and her hand trembles a little bit.

Joanna groans, but I know she loves it.

Hours later we're still getting ready. I've swapped out the blue cotton summer dress for one of red plush velvet. The neckline plunges down both the back and front, and the slit goes all the way up to reveal my entire right leg when I walk. I don't have much cleavage—Willow was always the one with the curves—but this dress works perfectly on my shape. It's by far the sexiest thing I've ever worn, and for the first time, I allow myself to draw power from it.

It's not something I would normally wear, but when Joanna pulled it out and dared me to wear it, I couldn't resist. It's the kind of dress that gets attention, and tonight, I want attention. From one man only. But I've noticed that when other men pay attention to me, Ryne reacts strongly.

My skin has paled in winter, which contrasts nicely against the red. Elle does my hair up in a swirl of soft curls, and Abi applies my makeup, complete with blood-red lips and smokey eyes. I've even learned how to walk in high heels, so I slip into some strappy black ones that will make me tower above the other girls.

Elle leans down to whisper in my ear so the other girls can't hear. They're distracted with their own dresses anyway. "Ryne isn't going to be able to keep his eyes off of you. Maybe tonight he'll come to his senses."

I have no idea what she's talking about, or why she's even saying this, though I do wonder if maybe she's been trying to convince him to not reject me. I still think she wants out of marrying him, and I'm her ticket to freedom.

I stand and examine myself in our full-length mirror. Before coming here, I would've felt self-conscious about how I look, especially about being so tall, but I don't care anymore. The wolves are massive men, anyway. I could never be taller than them. And I've decided that confidence makes me far prettier than all the hair and makeup and dresses combined.

"You're going to show Ryne what he's missing," Joanna laughs the second Elle leaves.

I smirk and blow a kiss to myself in the mirror. "That's the plan."

And okay, maybe some of this confidence is fake, and on the inside I'm terrified about so many things, but I have to at least try. Fact is, Ryne is my fated.

And I don't want to marry Nico.

I will if it's what I have to do to save myself from Anders or the mating houses, but part of me hopes that

Ryne will take one look at me and decide he doesn't want to marry Elle either.

A knock sounds on the door, and Madame Delphine slips into the room. "Poppy, this is a gift from Nico for you to wear tonight."

Joanna gasps. "I bet it's a family heirloom, same as what Grady gave me." She points to the gold necklace with the little flower of green emeralds on the end. "He said that wolves only give this type of jewelry to someone they consider part of their family." She winks and holds up her hands. "Just wait, soon we'll have engagement rings too."

Abi's smile is laced with pain. I can tell this hurts her, and I wish I could help. I vow then and there to do a better job of making sure she gets married to a beta too—a good one. Joanna and I still haven't told her that we're getting married soon, and that Ryne will be bringing a couple more betas into the season. I hope one of them is perfect for her.

I take the box from Madame Delphine and thank her. My hands shake when I slip the black ribbon from the box and peel it open. A gold necklace with a huge red sparkling stone in the shape of a teardrop winks up at me. My breath catches in my throat. I don't think I've ever seen something so beautiful.

"This is a ruby," Madame Delphine says wistfully. She clasps it to my neck. "It's a very rare and valuable gemstone. And Joanna is right. This piece belongs to

Nico and Anders's family. It's going to be a very exciting night for you."

Leave it up to Anders to have a gem that looks like a huge drop of blood.

But at least he wasn't the one who gave it to me. Thank goodness I'm going to be paired with Nico. But what has happened to Anders? Did Grady really go after him? And will Nico hate me once everything comes to light? Ready or not, I may soon find out. I swallow and keep my gaze away from Joanna, feeling guilty that she doesn't know Grady has made it his mission to end Anders.

We leave, and as we walk out to the river, the necklace weighs heavy.

CHAPTER 21

WE SHUFFLE ONTO THE BOAT, everyone trying to stay upright in our heels and tight dresses. We all look stunning tonight. Better even than on the night of the Wolf Moon Festival. All the girls understand what is at stake now, and we've gotten better at dressing ourselves and doing our makeup and hair. There are also attachments starting to form, real feelings involved for several of the girls and the betas. It's changed everything.

On the walk down to the dock, Faye eyed my and Joanna's necklaces but didn't say anything. She's the only one who doesn't look better than she did before. Her dress is a little too short and tight, and her makeup is a tad garish; her look reeks of desperation, and I'd feel bad for her if I didn't hate her so much. She's only gotten meaner through this experience, which is incredible considering how she started out. If I didn't understand her need to please the betas, I might judge her for it. But even despite our rivalry, despite the horrible things she's said about Willow, and even accusing me of killing Lexi, I still wouldn't wish her to end up in a mating house.

Though if it comes down to a beta for her or for Abi, I will fight for Abi. And the fact that the wolves have even put us into this position will never be okay. Once I'm married to Nico, I will find and join the Resistance. There's got to be a way to change things for the better. Even Ryne had a better idea about finding willing women to have the children, but I still don't like it. What's so bad about letting everyone get married?

The betas are nowhere to be seen. The sea air is cool, and we stand out on the dock much longer than usual. "Our hair is going to get messed up." Abi sighs. "Not that it matters for me, but I at least wanted them to get a look first."

Joanna laughs and pulls her into a hug.

A white boat finally putters around the corner, larger than any of the others I've been on. It has three stories, and the majority of the boat is enclosed with wide windows, though there is a walkway that seems to go all the way around the large interior room. The room has double doors that are intricately carved with gold trim. It comes in at a slow crawl and stops at the deck.

Another breeze kicks up, and goosebumps rise on my skin.

"Are they gonna let us in?" Joanna asks. "Or wait until we look a mess?"

This time Abi laughs.

Almost as if on cue, the doors open, and Knox stands on the other side wearing a tux. My heart flutters a little. I've never seen him so dressed up.

He meets my eye for a fraction of a second and then clears his throat. "Ladies, name cards have been placed at each table, so please find your seat. Ryne and the betas will be here soon."

Joanna grabs my hand and drags me to the front. Sure enough, we're sitting at a round table with six name cards. Mine, Joanna, Grady, Nico, Ryne, and Elle. Nico's name card is on my left, and Ryne's is on my right. I don't know why he would put himself right next to me, but perhaps he didn't have anything to do with the seating arrangements.

Abi is stuck at a table with Faye, Joy, and Blair. I know she'd much rather be with us or even Harlow and Katelyn. I mouth "I'm sorry" to her, and she just shrugs. She's used to it, and it's not fair. I don't know why I've received so much attention from all these betas, but it must be because I'm Ryne's fated mate. The men are probably picking up on something there, thinking I'm more special than I am. If I weren't Ryne's fated, I can't help but think I'd be at the mating house by now. I could even be pregnant.

A side door opens, and even before I see Ryne, I

know he's there. I can feel his presence like an electric current, and all of my senses heighten. The connection is stronger than ever. The men all enter, each dressed in identical black tuxes. Ryne strides in last.

His cobalt eyes meet mine, and it's as if the rest of the room disappears. It's only me and him. He doesn't move from the door; he just drinks me in, and I let him. I want to get up and go to him, but even being entranced by him, I know better.

I wonder what he would do if I did. Would he kiss me or reject me? I suspect he'd kiss me. Even he can't deny it, and I understand now how hard it must be for him to resist.

A hand drops on my shoulder, breaking the spell. Nico leans in, pressing a soft kiss to my cheek before sitting down.

"You look lovely," he says.

"Thank you," I mutter, tearing my eyes away from Ryne. Which is a mistake, because they land right on Joanna and Grady, who are in the middle of a passionate kiss. I avert my eyes and look over at Nico.

He leans in. "I'm sorry I don't treat you like Grady does Joanna." His gaze flicks to the necklace, and his facade falters for a moment. This jewelry was meant for Nova, and we both know it.

I swallow. "It's okay. I'm not sure I want you to."

Hurt crosses his face, but so does understanding.

This is such a hard position to be in. Still, I don't want to hurt his feelings.

"Yet," I hurry to say. "We're not there yet. You're still in love with Nova, and I would never want to take those feelings away from you."

He scoots a little closer to me and rests his arm along the back of my chair, his fingers lightly resting on my shoulder. "Thank you for being so considerate. The more I get to know you, the more I understand why Nova liked you so much." He pauses for a long second. "You're kind, and in this world there's not a lot of that, you know?"

I do know.

"I can't give you the feelings I gave so easily to Nova," he continues. "It's not in my power, and for that I apologize."

"You don't have to."

"Please, I need to say this." His voice is earnest.

I nod once, hoping whatever he says doesn't make this harder.

"I like you. You're my friend. And I wouldn't be doing this if I didn't really believe that in time, we will grow to love each other. I'd really like for us to have that chance."

"I would too," I say, but I know it's a lie.

Loving him would be like loving a shadow.

Ryne slides into the chair next to me, and I swear the temperature in the room rises by twenty degrees. I can't move, can't breathe. Did he hear our conversation?

"You look beautiful tonight, Joanna," he says, but his eyes are on me, and I know the compliment is mine. My cheeks flame, and I grab the glass of ice water and gulp it down. "Grady is a lucky man," he adds.

"The luckiest," Joanna quips back. "And I'd say the same of Elle if you weren't busy stripping another girl naked in your mind."

"Joanna!" Grady gasps, but Ryne just chuckles and leans back in his chair like it's all a silly little game of breaking hearts.

I'm mortified, about ready to strangle Joanna, and poor Nico shifts uncomfortably in his seat, his eyes going from me to Ryne and back again. I reach out and thread Nico's fingers through mine and squeeze. After a few long moments, he squeezes back. He can't know about me and Ryne. He'll break off the engagement. I'm sure of it. Or will Ryne make him marry me? He can't deny his alpha. Still, I don't want to risk anything.

Elle has been busy chatting with the other house mothers who are seated in the back, but unfortunately that couldn't last forever. When she saunters over and sits down next to Ryne, my heart drops. He leans over, whispering intimately in her ear, and she giggles. This is pure torture. Is that what I have in store for the rest of my life? I can only hope Nico and I won't have to be around the alpha too often.

Anders strolls up to Abi's table, finding his seat between Faye and Blair. He immediately pulls Faye into a kiss, and I relax a little. At least his gaze isn't on me. I don't think I could handle another beta's attention right now.

But I can't help but wonder what Anders knows or what happened between him and Grady. He obviously didn't succeed in killing Joanna two nights ago, but that doesn't mean he won't try again.

The water outside the boat twinkles under the moonlight and then ripples when the engine turns up. In the inky blackness of it, I imagine Nova's body floating aimlessly. Anders knows what really happened to her that night because he did it. What kind of person drowns someone like that?

The kind who decapitates a girl in front of her own family for no good reason.

The kind who bites a woman against her will, brandishing her for a date.

The kind who thinks women were made for men's enjoyment and nothing else.

We pull out into the water, and everyone cheers. I can't. All I can do is watch Anders, a glare deepening my gaze.

Anders meets my challenge through the midst of raised glasses and cheering, and we stare at each other. His handsome, charismatic face goes flat. There's nothing good behind his eyes. It's all fake. His expression is dark, clinging to mine. Neither of us turn away; neither of us break the spell. It's like we're in a face-off. He may be a beta wolf and used to this kind of thing, but I've spent my life fighting to survive in a terrible world. I'm no longer scared of a challenge.

And I'm no longer scared of Anders.

He nods once, raises his glass to me, and drinks.

He knows I know.

He must.

CHAPTER 22

WAITERS COME AROUND POURING WINE, and I eagerly down my first glass. Alcohol is not something I drink much of, but I need it to take the edge off. I'd probably drink the whole bottle if I thought it would help me tonight, but I know it won't, and that's not who I am. I'm scared to lose control, even when I know I've never really had it. So I sit here, sipping my second glass of wine and trying to make small talk with Nico, all the while completely and utterly aware of Ryne by my side. It's all I can do to not look at him.

I'm not the only one who drank my first glass of wine like it'd disappear if I didn't. Both Ryne and Nico did as well.

Before long, everyone at our table is relaxed and laughing at Joanna's stories. Our delicious meal is followed up by the most decadent dessert I have ever seen. It's a ball of chocolate mousse topped with fancy whipped cream. The richness of the chocolate sits heavy in my mouth. We never had anything like this back home, never had these kinds of parties or dresses or fancy food, but at least we were mostly free to do as we pleased within the confines of our community.

I sigh, the past really is gone. This is my life now, and I want so badly to believe it'll be a good one.

"Dinner parties with you two are going to be a riot," Elle says, her voice sweet and sultry like the chocolatey dessert, and my stomach sours. She glances around the table. "I like this group. After the weddings, we should make this a weekly occurrence." So much for avoiding the alpha.

Joanna raises her glass. "Definitely. To friendship."

We all raise our glasses and utter the same words. Ryne slides his free hand over mine in my lap under the table. He squeezes my fingers, and blood rushes to my face. I want to pull away and tell him to not toy with my feelings.

But of course I can't.

He lets go quickly and stands, moving to the front of the room. Elle slides into his vacated seat. She leans over and whispers into my ear. "It's going to be okay."

I stare at my hands. "I don't see how."

She reaches over and squeezes one of them, so utterly similar to the way Ryne did but carrying a very different meaning.

I can tell she craves her freedom. And she said herself that she didn't want to marry Ryne because she was worried she'd end up married to a man with a mistress. I don't know if that will ever happen—I don't want it to happen—but how can she be so calm about the situation now?

Ryne stands on a slightly raised platform in the front of the room. His presence is so commanding that the entire room quiets before he even looks up. When he does, he smiles, and my heart melts a little bit. I want that smile to be mine. And for a fraction of a second, it is. As he shifts his eyes across the room, they hold with mine and then drop away. Pretty indicative of our entire relationship, and I'm a lost cause. How can I possibly marry Nico when I feel like this?

"Wolves and ladies, tonight I brought you here to celebrate with me. You see, a few weeks ago, I was reunited with a dear friend of mine that I wasn't expecting to see. I'd always known I'd fall in love with her, but I didn't expect it to happen so quickly." His words are rushed and rehearsed, but they still sting. I steal a quick glance at Elle. She's smiling, but it doesn't reach her eyes. "Tonight, I'm announcing my engagement. Elle, can you join me up here?"

As she makes her way up to the stage, she's the picture of grace, and every eye is on her. When she reaches Ryne, she slides a petite arm around his waist. They're the perfect couple. She's all feminine beauty, and he's masculine power. They're gorgeous and strong and everything the pack wants.

"This is my lovely bride-to-be. We shall be married at the Pink Moon Festival." Cheers erupt around the room, and Ryne holds a hand out for quiet. "I have two more weddings to announce."

Whispers spread at those words. Ryne clears his throat, and everyone quiets. "This has been an unusual year for the claiming, and so when two of my betas came and asked for permission to marry their brides early, I couldn't deny them that, especially considering how I feel for Elle. I know what it's like to desperately want to be with someone."

The tension in the room rises as the girls realize two of the betas are about to be unavailable. I can feel the eyes on our table, and my skin prickles. Is it too late? Should I stand up right now and announce that I can't marry Nico? I want to, and yet I'm frozen in place.

"But I also didn't want to have a disappointing year at the harvest festival, so at the pink moon I will be bringing two new betas to take brides this autumn." That's the news everyone wants to hear, and several of the girls clap and squeal. "Now, it's time to announce the additional weddings. Grady and Joanna."

"No surprises there," someone mutters from the table behind me.

"And Nico and Poppy."

A collective gasp circles the room followed by a shattering glass. I search for the noise and see Anders standing up, his face beet red.

"You can't do that," he shouts. "They are not fated."

Ryne clenches his fists. "Are you challenging me?"

Anders doesn't move from his spot, but his chest rises and falls rapidly. "Of course not. But you know how I feel about Poppy. You can't let my son marry her. That's needlessly cruel."

I snort at his use of the word cruel.

"Why not?" Nico stands, his arms rippling with fur. I'm afraid we're about to see a bloodbath on this boat, which now seems far too small.

"Because it's a slap to my face, and I won't allow it. Poppy is mine." Anders storms toward us. "I claimed her the day I killed her sister. She's the reason I even entered the harvest this year, and you know it."

I expect Nico to move between me and Anders, but it's Grady who gets there first.

"What are you doing?" Anders asks, peering around him to meet my eyes. There is nothing but hatred and lust in them. The two emotions shouldn't go together, but for Anders they do, and they probably always will.

"I won't let you hurt Poppy," Grady snarls. He stands taller, and the two of them face off, ready to rip each other apart.

"What makes you think I want to hurt her?" he asks. "I love her."

A muscle in Grady's jaw ticks. "Go sit back down, old man. She's Nico's now."

Anders moves so quickly that I don't even register it. He grabs Joanna by the arm, wrenching her out of her chair. "Perhaps I'll take your bride instead then."

Grady leaps onto the table, sending plates and glasses flying, and then he's on top of Anders, punching him hard in the face. Blood flies, splattering the white linens. Anders releases Joanna and kicks out at Grady, slamming him in the gut. Grady doubles over for just a moment before tackling Anders to the ground. A flash of fur ripples over both of them in light gray and dark brown. They're going to shift any second. If that happens, this probably won't end until one of them is dead.

Ryne leaps from the platform and yanks Grady off of Anders. "Enough," his voice bellows. Anders stands, wiping blood from his mouth.

"That's insubordination," Anders says. "I am second in command to the alpha. You cannot attack me."

Ryne levels a look at him. "Be reasonable. You provoked him."

Not to mention, Anders questioned his alpha.

"That is no excuse. You know the punishment for insubordination. Are you going to be a strong alpha and enforce the rules, or will you let chaos reign?"

Ryne swallows, and I see the indecision in his mind.

"What's the punishment?" I whisper to Nico.

"Exile." The word seems to echo through the space, but that's only because everyone else is whispering the same thing.

My stomach drops. I don't want my friends to be sent away, because surely Joanna would go with him. The wilds are dangerous. I'd never see them again.

Joanna's face turns frantic, and my heart hurts to see a side of her I've never seen before. She's suddenly vulnerable and small, just like the rest of us women in this world. There's nothing left to do. I have to be strong.

"I'm sorry," I whisper to Nico. I still don't know what this is going to do to him, and I hate that he's already been through so much. He questions me with a small frown. But I'm out of time.

I step forward, point at Anders, and my voice finds me. "You killed my twin sister, Willow. My best friend and other half. That does not make me yours."

He laughs, and everyone turns on me. "It brought you here, didn't it?"

I won't be bated. "And you killed Nova. And you killed Lexi. And you tried to kill Joanna."

The silence is filled with so many emotions.

I hold Anders's gaze as he glares. Finally, he speaks, but his voice doesn't carry its normal tone. "You're a liar. How dare you accuse me of such things."

"I'm not a liar." My voice is all steel now; it holds me up, and I stand straighter because of it. "And I can prove it."

I reach out my right hand, and in it, Joanna places the rose that she's been keeping tucked in her bodice. She insisted on bringing it along tonight, just in case something like this happened. The rose itself is shriveled and sad looking since it was cut days ago, but it's intact well enough to serve its purpose. The second Anders's eyes land on it, he takes a step back. That small movement is not enough for most people to even notice, but I do, and I bet Ryne and the other wolves do as well.

"Do you recognize this?" I ask. "Wait, don't answer that; it wasn't really a question. I know you do because it was the very same rose you placed on your lapel on our date to the theater."

"What does that have to do with anything?" he scoffs. He looks over to Ryne. "Are you really going to let this go on?"

Ryne raises an eyebrow as if amused, but his eyes are filled with lead, the blues of them going dark. "Let the woman finish. If you're as innocent as you say you are, then you shouldn't have anything to worry about."

"That's ridiculous. No innocent man would tolerate being accused of murdering a claimed girl and his son's fated." He looks to Nico, expression pleading. "You know I loved Nova."

The color in Nico's complexion is gone. He's completely ashen. "No, Father, I never knew that. It was actually the opposite, as I recall."

"Hmm." Ryne takes a step closer. "Isn't that interesting?"

I clear my throat. "As I was saying..." I give the men a look as if to say *let me have my moment* and continue on. "This very rose was left behind when a wolf pretended to be a lycan and attacked Joanna on the night of the full moon."

Grady widens his stance. "Which I've known about for a whole twenty-four hours. You're lucky you're not already dead, and don't think I didn't try to find you because I did. I should've known you'd be spending the night at the mating houses again." He spits on the ground.

Anders glares right back. "This is preposterous. All that because of a rose?"

"There's more," I hiss. "You had a motive to kill Nova. You told me yourself that you hated that your son wouldn't be able to have children with her."

"Nova was depressed. She drowned herself." He tugs at his collar and sweat forms on his forehead.

I shake my head. "She was excited to marry Nico. That very night she told me she loved him." I turn back and point to poor Nico. He's still stunned. "Everybody knew how much you two loved each other—you most of all."

Abi steps forward, and it's maybe the first time anyone's ever paid her attention.

"Oh, what now?" Anders snaps.

"Lexi was my roommate. She was the top of our class, the smartest of the bunch, but you didn't think she was pretty enough to be a beta's wife."

Anders gapes at her. Of all people, I'm certain he never expected Abi to have something to say.

"Don't try to deny it," Abi continues. "She told me herself that you said she'd never be a beta wife. Well, maybe you made sure of it."

"I did no such thing." He points to Abi. "For all we know, you killed Lexi."

"That's not possible," I interject. "Her wounds were from claws and teeth, and it wasn't a full moon."

That's all it takes. Grady and Nico exchange a glance, and then together, they lunge for Anders.

CHAPTER 23

PANDEMONIUM ERUPTS.

Elle is at my side in seconds, grabbing my hand. I reach for Joanna, and we run for the back of the room. There's nowhere to go. Tables and chairs are flying as the betas all shift into their wolf forms. Girls huddle along the walls in groups. Elle stands between me and Joanna and the wolves. Every once in a while, I see her fur ripple along her arm.

"What are you doing?" I demand.

"Protecting you. All of this is about protecting you," she hisses in my ear. "Ryne and I aren't really getting married, and neither are you and Nico. We have a plan to keep you safe from Thorn, but we have to pretend like everything is normal until the last possible second. Ryne would be heartbroken if anything happened to you, so I'm making sure you stay safe."

I grip her arm, my mind still trying to catch up to what she confessed. "What plan?"

"I can't tell you."

I'm momentarily distracted by the howling wolves. Ryne gets himself between Anders and Nico, with Grady right by Nico's side. The other betas stand with Ryne. No one wants a bloodbath. But then again, they're used to that, and they'll do what they have to.

Without warning, Nico leaps over Ryne, landing on Anders, his jaws clamping on the back of his father's neck. Anders bucks, but Nico doesn't let go. He claws at Anders's face, and Anders rolls, pinning Nico underneath him. All the other betas join the fray, and for a moment all we can see is fur and gnashing teeth.

The wolves freeze.

"Anders just conceded." Elle breathes a sigh of relief, but she doesn't move away from shielding me.

The fur all changes to flesh, and now six naked men stand in the middle of the room, all breathing heavily. I keep my eyes on their heads and faces so I can concentrate on what they are saying.

Nico clenches his fist. "I do not accept that. You will die for killing Nova. How could you do that to me? Your own son."

"I concede," Anders repeats. "I will not fight my child like this. You can take my place as the alpha's second in command."

"That is acceptable to me," Ryne says loudly.

"Not to me," Nico growls. "And besides, that honor should go to Grady, shouldn't it? I won't be placated with false prizes." He points at his father, pain twisting his features. "I've lived under your claw for my entire life, doing everything you asked of me, and when the one thing came along that would actually make me happy, you had to take it away."

Anders's lips thin. He's not sorry. He's only sorry he got caught. He shakes his head at his son. "You never lived up to your potential, and you never will without my help."

Nico's face falls.

"There will be a trial," Ryne snaps in response. "We will bring King Tremaine in to exercise judgment, but for now, nobody is killing anybody."

Nico looks from Ryne to Anders and then storms off. Grady has been holding Anders, but now he lets him go, striding over to Joanna and wrapping her in a hug. He's still naked as the day he was born, but they obviously don't care. Elle shoots me a knowing look and rushes forward, picking up a couple of tablecloths. She hands them to the men and then gives one to me. "Take this to Nico to cover himself."

I take the stained white sheet and hurry out the door where I last saw Nico. He's leaning against the railing and staring down into the water. I approach and hand him the tablecloth. He takes it without a word and wraps it around his midsection.

"Are you okay?" I ask.

He shakes his head. "I can't believe my own father would kill her."

I lay my hand on his arm. "I'm so sorry."

His face crumples, and he collapses into me, sobbing. This isn't something I ever thought I'd see from one of these tough men, but it doesn't bother me. If anything, it makes me like him more. He's a good man, and he never deserved any of this. I hold him and stroke his hair, not caring that he's ruining my dress or that he's half-naked. Nico is my friend, and he's hurting.

I hope that at some point, Anders feels pain worse than this.

It would be the only way justice could be served.

***

The boat docks roughly at the city's edge, and we all scramble off. I want to get far away from the betas and all the trouble they bring. Plus, I need to get away from Anders. I'm the one who accused him, and I'm fairly certain he'll come after me the first chance he gets.

So when I see him being led away by Cade and Justin, I relax a little.

"Where are they taking him?" I ask anyone who might be listening.

"To the jail cells. He'll stay there until the king comes to render judgment," Elle says. "Normally this would be Ryne's choice, but Anders is ranked high enough that he gets to plead his case to Thorn."

At least I don't have to worry about Anders for now, but the thought that Thorn will be here soon makes my skin crawl.

"Elle, Poppy, you're coming with me," Ryne calls out. It's not a request; it's a command.

"Why?" I ask, now concerned. Elle shrugs, and we head for his car. Joanna watches me with worried eyes, but Grady is already ushering her to his own car.

We pile into the backseat of Ryne's car, Elle pressed up against him. I shove down my jealousy. "Why do I need to come with you?"

Ryne doesn't look at me. "You're the one who accused Anders of murdering two women. I want to hear the story from you. I need to know exactly what happened."

"The night Nova died . . ." I start.

"Not here," he whispers, his voice cracking with exhaustion. "Wait until we get back to my house, and I've cleaned up a bit."

I glance up at the rearview mirror and find Knox's eyes on me. Obviously Ryne doesn't trust Knox with this information, but I'm not sure why. Maybe he's just being careful, or maybe he really does want to get cleaned up first.

We arrive at his house, and Ryne heads up to what I assume is his room as Elle leads me to another bedroom.

It's beautiful with white silk blankets across a large bed and intricately painted landscapes on the walls. She opens up a drawer and pulls out a black top and shorts similar to what we run in.

"Why do you have clothes here? I thought you stayed at the house."

"I actually sleep here more often than not lately." She hands me the clothes. "Here, you need to get out of that dress."

I glance down at what was once a beautiful dress that is now splattered with blood. I didn't even realize it got on me. I change quickly, and so does she. Then she leads me to another room on the floor. It's a library, but smaller than the one at the claimed house. Dark shelves line all four walls from floor to ceiling; there are no windows. A small table sits in the middle of the room, framed by four squashy leather chairs.

Elle examines a shelf near the door and plucks out a book. "Good luck," she says, moving for the door.

"You're not staying?" I ask.

"No. This is between you and Ryne. He wants you to be able to speak freely about what you know. Good night, Poppy. I'll see you in the morning." She winks as she leaves, which confuses me even more.

If her confession is true, then she must care for him as a friend more than anything else, and she did say that she wasn't really going to marry him. I think about Knox. We used to date, and I even thought I loved him, but I know now that we were only ever meant to be friends. Still, I'd do anything to help him.

Maybe that's how Elle feels about Ryne.

I walk around the room slowly, looking at the books on the built-in shelves. I can read all of the titles now. Sure, I might be slow, but I can do it, and pride fills me more and more with each one. These last months have been the hardest of my life, but at least I have something to show for it. I take a book from the shelf titled *Persuasion* and flip through a few of the pages. Okay, maybe this one might take me a while, but I'm intrigued by the first line, which seems to go on and on forever. I didn't know people could write like that. Maybe I could write something one day. Would I share the story of my life? Or would I want to make up something else entirely? A magical land where none of this horror exists.

The door creaks open, and I turn, meeting Ryne's stormy eyes. He still isn't wearing a shirt, and his pants hang low on his hips. He shuts the door and locks it. Ryne and I have never been so alone before, not with a locked door and no windows. A jolt of nervous excitement pulses through my entire body.

Ryne approaches me. I expect him to say something, anything. He doesn't. He places a finger on my chin and forces me to look up at him. Then his lips are on mine. They are rough and hungry as he presses his body into me, pushing me back into the bookshelf.

I drop the book I'm holding and wrap my arms

around him, ignoring the wooden bookshelf biting into my back. This is the kiss I've been waiting for. It holds the promise of future and love.

And then I remember.

He's engaged to Elle.

I shove him away from me.

"Are you going to marry Elle?" I breathe. He can't kiss me until he explains himself.

He chuckles and closes the distance between us, planting a kiss on my nose. "That's a ruse," he says. He grabs my hand with his and leads me over to one of the chairs. He sits, and when I go to sit in the opposite chair, he growls a little and pulls me into his lap.

"I don't understand," I say, but I think I'm starting to, and my hope feels too good to be true.

He nuzzles my neck. "I don't want to talk tonight, Poppy. I just want to be with you."

And here I thought he brought me here to talk about Anders.

His lips feather along my jaw, and it takes all of my willpower to not melt into him. But I need answers first.

"I really need to understand what's going on. You've been ignoring me since the night you admitted we are fated." My heart hurts at the memory.

He squeezes me tighter. "I know. I'm so sorry I've kept my plan a secret from you. It's been so difficult. You have no idea how many times I've come close to ravishing you in front of everyone."

"Then why haven't you?" The words are out of my mouth before I can stop them.

He grins, and his eyes dance. "You would've liked that, huh?"

I nod because my words seemed to have escaped me at the moment.

"Because you'd be in danger from my father. Unlike Anders, he doesn't have to hide his kills. You threaten my relationship with Elle, something he's planned for years, and I have no doubt he'll kill you if he finds out."

I place my hands on his chest, spreading my fingers over the hard muscles.

"So, what's the plan?" I ask.

"Oh, it's quite brilliant. Elle came up with it. The night of the wedding, you and Elle will switch at the last possible moment, and I'll marry you instead. It's part of our shifter bond that we cannot attack another's wife, so once you're mine, my father won't be able to touch you."

A thrill races up my spine. His wife.

"What about Elle and her family?" I can't forget everything she told me about how important this marriage is to them.

"They will all be here for the wedding. And just before the ceremony, I'll initiate Elle and her family into our pack. They will have to move here, but at least they'll be protected. Thorn won't want to mess with that. Besides, it's not like any of this is Elle's fault. We're going to make it look like it was all my doing and that Elle wasn't part of the plan. My father will pity her and will be angry at me, but he won't retaliate. Oh, he'll make threats, but I'm his only heir and the child he spent decades trying to have." His face softens. "Trust me, Poppy. Everything will be okay once the dust settles."

What is it with these men and their terrible fathers? It makes me miss mine even more. I can't imagine ever having to go to such lengths to keep Papa from hurting the people I care about. I frown, overcome with immense sadness for Ryne. He deserves so much better.

"I hope it works." I don't know what else to say.

"Me too." He runs the back of his hand gently along my jawline. "You understand that after we leave this room, we have to go back to ignoring each other until the festival, and even there, we really can't even look at each other until the moment you and Elle switch places?"

"I understand."

"Good, now can we please stop talking?"

CHAPTER 24

THOSE BLUE EYES glitter with mischief and then flash deeper. Longing is evident on his face as he inches his body closer to mine, and there's nothing else to say or do. I reach out and pull him close, erasing any distance between us. His mouth takes mine, and a fire ignites between us. It's hotter than it's ever been before, and I'm happy to let it burn me up. The kiss is zero to one hundred in seconds, as if we're fighting to stay alive, and the only way to do so is to stay connected.

Ryne is everything.

He works his lips against mine, and it's like the whole world is falling away. My heart is burning with a passion that makes me feel like a whole different person—like the women in our village right after they got married. They always had a way about them, as if losing their virginity gave them a knowledge and maturity the rest of us couldn't understand. And maybe that was true, or maybe that was just a shield, but I never cared. It didn't interest me. I knew one day I'd marry too and would leave my maidenhood behind, but I'd hardly thought about it much.

Now it's all I can think about.

I've never wanted someone or something as much as I want Ryne.

He must feel the same, because we go from me straddling him on the chair to him straddling me on the floor. He lifts from me for a moment, breaking the kiss, and I murmur my frustration.

He chuckles, and it's a lovely kind of wickedness. "What am I going to do with you?"

"I have a few ideas." I reach up to bring him back to me, but he holds strong, still leaning over me and caging me to the floor with those steel arms. I don't know how he can possibly wait. His hair hangs down to frame his face, so I shimmy my hands free and run my fingers through it.

He groans and rolls away.

"What's wrong?" I ask, teasing. But part of me is afraid that something really is wrong. If he rejects me now, I might die of heartbreak.

"We can't do anything but kiss, and I'm dying." He lets out a laugh.

"So if you die, then we'll die together." I move close and trail slow kisses along his neck. I've never felt so bold before, but I like it. "Because I feel the same way."

"The claimed girls have to stay virgins until marriage."

I roll my eyes. "Are you serious?" My mom drilled innocence and virtue into us until she was blue in the face, but none of that really mattered to me, and it certainly doesn't now. "We're going to be married in three weeks anyway. What's the difference?" He turns and kisses me again, long and deep, and I think he's agreed until he pulls away once more. "We don't have to tell anyone," I whisper.

And what I don't say is that I hardly think it's fair for any of these men to insist their wives come to the marriage beds as virgins considering their pastimes in the mating houses.

"It doesn't work like that," he says. "I wouldn't want to keep this a secret from my brothers in the pack. It's very hard to lie to each other because once we're in our wolf forms, so much comes through the link between us."

"I don't understand."

"We work together as a whole. Could your left hand lie to your right hand?"

"Oh . . ."

"Which is why I didn't want you to know about our future marriage until the last possible second. It's hard enough for me and Elle to keep this a secret. What if I slipped, and it got out to others? Or let's say you told Joanna, and she told Grady.–"

"You can trust Grady."

"I know. He's one of my closest friends, but it's not so simple."

"You're the alpha. Make it simple."

He growls a little and tugs me closer, placing a kiss on my temple. "And here I thought you were sweet and innocent. You're conniving."

But he's laughing, so I snuggle in closer to him—as if that were possible. "You can't blame me for that. You're the one who threw me in a house with twenty other girls and said, 'Fight for a man.' Of course I've learned to be ruthless. I didn't want to end up in a mating house."

His grip tightens on me for a moment, and then he wiggles away and stands, helping me up. Once I get a little distance, my mind clears, and I'm reminded of all the things I want to ask him. I wouldn't be able to live with myself if I didn't speak my truth.

"Ryne, why don't you make changes around here? You're the alpha. You said yourself that you wanted the mating houses to be filled with women who are there willingly, so why not do it?"

His face softens, eyes dropping to the floor.

"What's more, why not do away with the claiming altogether? The women who wants to come to the shifters city to date the wolves for a chance at a better life could, and if it didn't work out, they could either willingly go to the mating house as a means of employ-ment, or they could return home. I've been thinking about this a lot, and I can't leave here tonight without letting you know my feelings."

His eyes pop up, and he hugs me. "I wish it were that easy."

"So that's a no?" My voice cracks.

"It's a beautiful dream, Poppy. But it's not the reality of this world."

"So what? You send innocent girls to the mating houses against their will? And what about you, do you go there? Do you sleep with women who would like nothing more than to live a normal life?"

I already know he does. He took me to one and said as much.

He lets out a long sigh. "You're right. I know that. And I would love nothing more than to be able to give you that world one day and prove myself a worthy alpha on my own terms." He takes my hands in his. "Poppy, I lied to you. I often go to the mating houses to check on the women, but I've never been with one of them like that. Not every wolf in my pack has, and I don't enforce it. Some of us don't believe in having sex with someone placed in a whorehouse against her will, even if that woman acts like she wants to."

I gape at him. Why would he keep this a big secret? All those lies to protect his image? "Ryne, this is huge. We need to talk about this."

He shakes his head. "No. It's time to go back. We've got three weeks, and then we can talk all you like." He gently kisses my lips again. "Until then, we can't let anything jeopardize the plan. Thorn will be here in less than a week to take care of Anders. I already sent a few wolves to fetch him. He's the biggest danger to you, so I'll make sure Elle keeps you close. That way, when my eyes are inevitably drawn to you, he'll think I'm looking at her."

I smile. "Now who's the conniving one?"

He kisses me once more. "You have to go."

I pull him close. "Sure, I'll go."

Three kisses later, and we still haven't left the library.

The next morning at breakfast, Joanna sets her plate down next to mine. "What the hell happened last night?"

I flush, and my eyes flick up to Elle, who sits across the table from me. "What do you mean? Nothing happened."

Joanna raises an eyebrow. "You mean, you just went to Ryne's house and spent hours there, and nothing happened?"

"How do you know I spent hours there?"

"Because I ran into Abi when I got here, and she said you didn't come home until two in the morning."

I feel my face flaming once again as my mind flashes back to a particularly passionate kiss and Ryne's hands wandering where I'd never let a man go before.

"Why are you blushing?"

"I'm not blushing." My voice has taken on a dreamy quality, and normally I'd give in to her by this point.

"Yeah, you are. Hello! You're as red as your namesake." Then she looks at Elle, who's staring at us from across the room, and visibly swallows. "I see. We'll talk about this later."

I can't talk about it later. I promised Ryne. "There's nothing to talk about. Ryne questioned me for a while. Elle was there. I'm blushing because he's intimidating to be around, and I'm embarrassed about the whole situation. I'm not used to having his undivided attention. He wanted to know everything I know about the deaths and the attack on you."

I hate lying, but I want Ryne's plan to work. Nobody can know.

She twists that around in her mind for a long minute before relaxing. "Yeah, Grady's all up in arms about it. He and Ryne are going to question Anders this morning. Ryne showed up at our door bright and early, telling Grady he wants to understand everything before King Tremaine gets here."

Morning classes pass in a blur, and Joanna stops

questioning me. Maybe she bought the story, or maybe she didn't, and we simply haven't had any more alone time for her to continue her interrogation. Either way, I'm glad to be free of it. I'll tell her everything after the Pink Moon Festival, but I can't say anything until then.

I wish I could. I want nothing more than to gush to my best friend about my man.

She catches me on the way to lunch. "The weather's nice. You want to grab our food and eat outside?"

A warning signals in my head. "Yeah, that sounds good. We'll get Abi and Elle to come as well."

She nudges me. "No, silly. Just you and me."

I don't know what I'm going to tell her. I'm not good at keeping things from her, but I can't say anything.

I'm still trying to figure out how to keep lying to Joanna when the front door flies open. Ryne stands there flanked by two men I've never seen before. "That's her," he says, his voice dark and angry, and points right at me.

Adrenaline slices through me like a knife.

The men descend on me, and I have a momentary thought to run, but none of this makes sense. I freeze. But they don't touch me. Instead they grab Joanna.

She struggles against their grip. "Let me go," she demands.

Ryne stalks toward her. "You're part of the Resistance," he spits.

I knew there was a Resistance, but it's the first I've heard of it from him. My heart rips itself in two at that moment, half with my mate and half with my friend. Because I know what he speaks is the truth. But after what he confessed last night, doesn't he understand why the Resistance even exists? Is he really so surprised and angry that women would try to take down this horrible system?

She glowers at him. I expect her to deny it, but that's never been Joanna's style. "Oh yeah? Prove it."

Another figure appears at the door, and I crane my neck around so I can see him. My blood runs cold. Anders.

He saunters into the room, a free man. "Funny that. I uncovered a group of Resistance women, and as per King Tremaine's instructions, I took care of them without bothering Ryne. The king felt it was best to work under the radar on this one. Of course I was forced to tell Ryne the whole story this morning." He winks at Joanna. "You were my last target. I actually didn't plan on killing you right away. I planned on questioning you first to see if you could help me find the head of the movement and lead me to more kills. But as you know, Elle got in the way."

"You're lying," Joanna shouts, her eyes locked on Anders in challenge. "You killed those women because you didn't approve of them. Nova wouldn't have given your son children, and Lexi wasn't good enough in your eyes to be a beta's wife."

"Oh really? Then why would I have come after you?"

"Same reason." But her voice waivers.

"Don't flatter yourself." Anders chuckles. "Oh well. You'll be dead soon enough. Maybe Thorn will still let me do the honors."

Ryne's eyes darken. "That's enough gloating from you, Anders. I don't approve of the way you handled this. But that doesn't change the fact that Joanna is part of the Resistance. It makes sense now." He glares at her. "Don't forget I caught you trying to run away."

"Doesn't she get a trial?" I rush forward, panic settling in. I can't see another sister—because that's what Joanna has become to me—killed by these men.

Ryne doesn't even acknowledge me, and suddenly it feels like everything is falling apart. "Take her to the prison," he orders. "King Tremaine is already on his way. With matters of the Resistance, he insists on taking things into his own hands. How unfortunate for you, Joanna. I may have shown a shred more mercy."

Joanna stares up at him, disbelief in her eyes. "Where's Grady?"

"Resistance or not, he'd fight for you. We had to lock him up. We'll let him out after we've dealt with you."

My mind can't seem to comprehend what is going on. "Dealt with her? What's that supposed to mean?" I ask.

"If she's found guilty, she'll be executed for treason."

"No, you can't do that." My voice shatters into a million broken pieces.

Ryne's eyes finally turn and plead with mine. "Please, Poppy, don't make this harder than it has to be."

"Then don't take my best friend away to prison."

"I don't have a choice."

Elle grabs one of my arms and Abi the other, moments before my knees give out. Then the men drag Joanna away.

For the first time since I've known her, she doesn't fight.

It's as if she knows she's already lost.

CHAPTER 25

I CAN'T HELP IT. I'm not usually much of a crier, but I keep finding myself in tears. I'm in that exact state when Elle comes and sits next to me at lunch days later. She wraps an arm around my shoulders but doesn't say a thing. Abi is on my other side, and she doesn't say anything either. But she gets it.

I can't eat. The words start to flow, an emotional catharsis that I can't stop once I start. "Ryne hasn't shown his face here for days, and nobody will tell us anything. Have they already sentenced her? Killed her? I have no idea what's going on. I hate this. It's wrong. Why won't anyone tell us anything?" I turn to Elle, pleading with her through watery eyes. "Do you know? Can you tell me?"

She shakes her head. "I don't know anything either."

Faye prances into the dining room. When she sees

the three of us, she stops short and snorts. "Oh, not this again."

"Shut up," I growl. I always knew she was a bitch, but this is over the line. I can't believe she's being so heartless about Joanna.

"You are so pathetic. You know that, right? My goodness, if I'd known all it took to get the attention of the betas was acting like a helpless victim, I would've taken notes."

"And you still would've sucked," Abi snaps. "Why do you always pick on Poppy? She never did anything to you!"

"Ha! Has the shy little mouse finally found her voice?" Faye mocks. "Please, go back to keeping your mouth shut."

"You're jealous of Poppy." Abi stands, her glossy black hair swinging behind her. "Don't you get it, Faye? This isn't about us versus us. It's about us versus them!"

"Now you sound like one of the Resistance." Faye raises an eyebrow. She does have a point, but there's no way Abi is a part of the Resistance. She's only a girl who's waking up to the truth, the same as all of us. "Hmm, I'm sure Anders would love to hear all about this conversation on our date tonight."

"I'm not Resistance." Abi swings her arms and points to the girls all staring up at the two of them battling it out. "None of us are. But what we are is trapped in a disgusting game, and we shouldn't be trying to hurt each other any more than the wolves already are."

"You're just saying that because you can't get one," Faye replies, stalking close to Abi and hovering over her. "And everyone knows it."

There's a chorus of laughter from the area where the distillery girls sit. I wipe a few tears away and watch both girls.

Abi lunges for Faye.

She wasn't a great fighter when she came here, but it turns out, Abi's a quick study.

They both land hard on the floor, Abi on top of Faye, punching her in the gut. These aren't slaps or hair pulling—none of the things of cat fights of the past— this is real hand-to-hand combat. We've been learning this over the last three months, but now we're seeing it in action.

Everyone jumps up, and the distillery girls come running. Faye screams and punches Abi in the mouth. Blood sprays from her lips, but Abi shakes it off and retaliates by breaking Faye's nose.

"Aren't you going to do something?" Blair screams at Elle, who is watching the whole thing with a smirk on her face.

Elle shrugs. "Looks like they're figuring it out just fine."

Actually, it looks like Abi is beating the snot out of Faye, and I've never been more proud. The rest of the distillery girls finally realize nobody is going to help their friend, so they jump in, and suddenly it's a full-on brawl.

Everyone is fighting.

I'm not about to be left out. I swing my leg around and get Blair right in the kidney; she goes down with a groan.

It feels. . . amazing. I actually feel like I'm doing something with myself. I go after Emma, and after a few good hits, she squeals and runs away. I turn, ready to take on my next opponent, but everyone's stopped.

"It's a damn good thing you're already spoken for," Madame Delphine says, storming in the room and pointing right at me. "Or else you'd be back to scraping the bottom of the leaderboard again. And right before a festival, no less."

"She started it." Raven points at Abi, and a bunch of the girls call out in agreement.

Abi peels herself off of a bruised and bloody Faye. "Not even going to try to deny it." She laughs bitterly. "I already know I'm going to end up in the mating house by the end of all this. Least I can do is ugly up Faye to make myself feel better." Abi brings a hand to her mouth, and I see her wiggle a few teeth.

Faye whimpers on the ground, her nose gushing blood, and her friends slowly help her up. She's going to have black eyes for weeks.

I hate that we keep fighting. Fighting each other isn't right. But some of these girls never seem to learn. They trade insults like they're ammunition. And quite frankly, I'm tired of it.

So is Abi.

Good for her. She's acting like Joanna, and I love every second of it. Joanna has been good for all of us. My eyes prick with tears. I don't even know if she is still alive.

"You'll be getting two new betas after the next festival." Madame Delphine frowns at Abi. "What if one of them takes a liking to you?"

Abi lifts a shoulder. "Still worth it."

I hope she's right, but when everything is said and done, I have a feeling she'll change her mind.

Madame Delphine surveys the lot of us, disappointed. Except for Bailey and her book, we're all a mess. "Get yourselves cleaned up. We're going into the city tonight." She pauses for a minute, and the energy intensifies. "King Tremaine has arrived."

We get a front-row seat to Joanna's trial, but it feels like I'm walking into a funeral or another brawl where only one side can come out victorious. At least she's still alive, but it's likely she won't be for long. I'm so nervous my hands are shaking, and my stomach feels like it's been carved out with a knife. We are seated outside on long benches in front of a tall building. A double staircase leads to a landing flanked by tall columns. Underneath the landing is a set of double doors.

"What's that?" I ask, pointing at the ominous doors.

"The prison. Back before the war against the paranormal, it was a market. But the wolves bricked it all in and made it a prison for the humans who fought against them. Nowadays, it's hardly used," Elle said. "Most people who get into trouble here don't last long."

Madame Delphine stands next to Elle but doesn't add anything. She stares up at the landing where Ryne stands with Nico, Grady, and Anders. Anders is arguing with Grady, whose face is red, but Ryne is staring at me. I drop my eyes, and Elle squeezes my hand.

"Stay strong," she whispers in my ear.

A hand touches my shoulder, and I glance up to see Madame Delphine looking at me, her eyes full of concern.

"This isn't fair," I say.

"I know. But maybe she'll be acquitted. They have no proof."

I want to believe her, that they won't execute my best friend over a madman's accusations, but everything I've seen with these wolves has shown me otherwise. And what if they do have proof?

A collective howl erupts from the crowd behind us. A pretty car with dark windows has pulled up, and King Tremaine steps out from the passenger door. He's dressed in a dark suit with his hair slicked back—the picture of power and wealth. In another time I might have found him handsome, but knowing who he is makes him look harsh.

He heads up the stairs flanked by a couple of bodyguards. Thorn greets Ryne and the others with a handshake. Grady leans over and whispers something in Ryne's ear. He doesn't say anything back, but he frowns deeply, and his eyebrows furrow.

The king shakes off his jacket and looks over the crowd. It's larger than I expected. How often do they have trials like this? Maybe most of the wolves came to see the king. Or maybe they're here for blood.

The king stands at the edge of the platform and surveys us all. I wish there weren't a railing there because then all it would take was a small shove, and he'd fall to his death. Or maybe I'm being dramatic. It's not that far down.

He holds up a hand, and the crowd quiets.

"Friends, I seem to be making more trips than normal down here lately. Maybe I should relocate." A howl goes up again, and he chuckles. I glance over at Ryne, who does not look happy with that idea. "Today though, I'm here to celebrate with you. Anders, come join me, please." Anders moves to his side, and the king puts a hand on his shoulder. "Anders discovered a plot among some of our women to kill and overtake us. Not that they could possibly succeed, but they could hurt or kill a few of us, and every wolf's life is worth protecting."

That's a lie. If it were true , then they wouldn't fight to the death for dominance, but I have a feeling most of what is going to come out of his mouth is a lie. I haven't heard of the resistance movement wanting to kill the wolves. It's more about protecting the women. And maybe there's more to it--maybe there could be equality, and maybe the dream I confessed to Ryne could come true. I swallow that down though, because too much hope hurts even more than none.

"In the process of discovering this plot, he killed two of the women involved and found a third. I was called in to decide what we will do with this woman. I have decided that we will execute her to kick off the Pink Moon Festival, and all can watch. In the meantime, Anders will head up a group of wolves who will interrogate her to root out the rest of the women involved. I will stay in town and oversee the interrogation."

The breath rushes out of me. "No," I croak. "That wasn't a trial. She's not even here."

Elle grips my hand. "Keep quiet, or they'll think you're involved as well."

Movement up on the platform distracts me. Grady rushes for the king, and they both go over the rail and plummet to the cobblestones below.

Everyone reacts. Men descend on where the two fell. Ryne changes into his wolf and leaps off the balcony, landing in the middle of the crowd. He howls, and the surging crowd retreats. I can't see what's going on because there are too many people in the way.

I try to shove forward, but Elle and Madame Delphine hold me back. "You'll get trampled."

"But I have to know," I say.

"You'll find out soon enough."

I watch the writhing crowd as they all drop to one knee. Ryne still stands there in his wolf form, but another wolf stands next to him now. He's the same color as Ryne, midnight black, but he's almost twice as large. He howls, and the men in front of us shift into wolves as well, answering his call.

Of course, King Tremaine survived his fall.

But I doubt Grady will live much longer.

The two snarl at each other, and right as Grady pounces for the king, several of the wolves lunge. The alpha king howls, and the other wolves fall to the sides. They paw at the ground, eager to jump back into the fray, but for now they'll listen to whatever the king has ordered through the shifter link. I'm not sure if it's telepathy, intuition, or what exactly, but they understand each other so well in this form, and I'm left to stand here and watch.

At least Joanna isn't here to see it. Witnessing Grady's death would break her.

There's a moment of silence. It stretches tight like a wire. And then it snaps.

The king and Grady lunge at each other, snarling as

they do. Thorn's wolf is massive, but Grady is quick. He dodges Thorn's claws and gets a swipe of his own, then rolls away and jumps back up to do it again. Thorn isn't falling for it a second time. He catches Grady's paw between his teeth and bares down. Grady howls painfully. I think the arm is about to break, but the king stops, flips Grady over, and presses his other leg to Grady's neck.

Grady changes back, and then so does the king.

I look down, staring at my scuffed shoes not only because I don't want to witness their nudity, but more because I don't want to see my friend's death.

"Ryne!" the king calls out. "Grady here is your number three, is he not?"

"He is, Father," Ryne growls. Anger radiates from his voice, but still, I don't look. I can't look. I won't.

"Then why would he challenge me, his king and an alpha, if he is loyal to you? Is this your doing?"

"Never," Ryne spits. "He does it because Joanna is his fated mate." Ryne bows his head, subservient to the king.

"And you didn't even give her a chance to defend herself," Grady shouts.

Thorn chuckles madly. "Well then, that certainly makes things interesting. I was planning to kill you today for your insubordination, but I think it would be more fitting that you die at the full moon with your mate."

"I'd rather die for her than live for you," Grady

snaps, and Thorn presses his face into the floor until Grady coughs.

"Don't worry, that will be arranged. But since this is my son's pack, he will be the one to do it."

Ryne's face pales. "Father—"

"You will kill them yourself, Ryne, and you will do it in front of your pack like the alpha you were born to be. End of discussion!"

With that, he storms from the grounds, and Grady is hauled away.

CHAPTER 26

I CAN'T SLEEP. Soon, Joanna and Grady will be executed. It's been two days since the so-called trial, and everyone is acting like nothing is wrong. I throw on my workout clothes and plan to get a run in before the monotony of classes.

Not that I've been paying much attention. I can't. Not with Joanna's death looming. I'm slipping a little on the board, but at this point, I don't care. I'll be married off soon anyway.

Everyone's still sleeping, and the sun won't be up for another hour, but I tug on a jacket, then jog quietly down the stairs. I hear voices and freeze.

"This is wrong," Elle whispers, "and you know it."

"There's nothing I can do. He won't listen to me," Madame Delphine responds. I wish I could see them, but I stay right where I am. "We're not married anymore, and even when we were, he didn't listen to me. It's a good thing I gave him Ryne, or I might not even be alive today."

A hand slams against a wall. "Thorn is going to be the death of us all," Elle growls.

Madame shushes her and then sighs. "I know."

I peek around the corner and blink into the darkness, making out their forms. They don't see me, but the despondency is clear in both their voices.

Madame Delphine places a hand on Elle's arm, but she shakes herself free. "I can't take this anymore. I'm heading over to talk to Ryne. Thorn hasn't left his side, but he's never been an early morning person. We'll see if we can come up with a solution so that Grady and Joanna will live."

Madame Delphine slips back into her room, and Elle heads out the front door. I follow, and she still doesn't notice me, or if she does, she doesn't acknowledge my presence. Surely a wolf would hear someone following. They have a heightened sense of hearing, and Elle is a powerful luna. Maybe she wants me to trail after her, or maybe she's too lost in her thoughts.

She heads down the path to the boats. I keep to the bushes and trees and manage to follow her all the way to the river. A large ferryboat waits there. She climbs aboard and heads to the front to talk to the captain. Their voices murmur good-naturedly, and I use the distraction to slip aboard and hide underneath one of the benches. I have no idea what I'm doing, but Ryne loves me. He hasn't said it yet, but he doesn't have to. I know it's true. Maybe he'll listen to me. I have to see him and convince him to not hurt Joanna or Grady.

The floor is rough on my skin and smells faintly of fish, but this will be worth it. The bumpy ride seems to take forever, but eventually the boat stops at another dock. I peek out and see Elle and the captain disembarking from the front of the boat.

I sneak out from under my bench and hit the dock from the back side. There are a lot more boats out here, so I manage to hide in between them. It's early morning, and there's no one else around. Ryne's house is visible from the docks because it's on the other side of the park. I spot Elle walking through the greenery, her shoulders back and her head high. I keep to the shadows of the surrounding houses and manage to slip up the walk to his front door.

She knocks.

Now is the time to reveal myself. It's too late to turn back.

I hop up next to her. "Hey, Elle," I say brightly.

She squeaks and jumps from me, holding her heart. "Don't scare me like that."

"Sorry." But I'm not sorry. "And don't pretend like you didn't know I was following you all along."

"Hmm . . . no comment on that." She winks and then

narrows her eyes. "So I assume you're here for the same reason as me?"

"Yup. I overheard you and Madame Delphine. I wanted to talk to Ryne as well. If he gets mad that I'm here, you can always say I snuck along, and you had no idea I was following you."

Her lips quirk. "You're something else, Poppy." "

The front door opens, and Knox stands there, freshly showered and dressed for the day in his slacks and button up. He takes in both me and Elle, not appearing surprised to see us. His eyes linger on my face for a second longer than they should. Will we ever get to talk? And if we do, what will he say to me?

I know what I'll say to him. I'll say that I'm sorry he's in this position, I'm sorry that we can't be together, that he's become a slave to the wolves, and that I'll do what I can to make his life better. But I won't apologize for loving Ryne.

Because I do love him.

"It's not a good time," he whispers, snapping out of his trance. "Thorn is staying here."

"I was sort of hoping he'd be out at the mating houses all night," Elle replies. She takes a step back. "Let Ryne know we came."

She turns to leave.

"No," I hiss, "I need to talk to Ryne. Now."

Knox purses his lips. "Since when did you become so stubborn?"

It's not a compliment. My mouth drops open, but I recover quickly. "Since Willow died in front of me. Since you pretended not to know me. Since I found Nova's dead body. Since—"

"Wait, you two know each other?" Elle interrupts.

An awkward silence follows, and I know I've said too much. Knox clears his throat. "Same village. That's all."

"I'm not leaving." I fold my arms over my chest and widen my stance. "So go wake up Ryne and get his wolfy butt out here."

"No need." Ryne's voice breaks through the tension, and I jump. "Me and my wolfy butt are right here." He's bounding up the front steps from the street, shirtless and sweating. Gym shorts cling to his hips, but even his feet are bare. He must have been running in his wolf form this morning. My heart jumps at the sight of him, wanting to go to him, but he doesn't look happy to see me.

He peers around for a minute, and then his eyes land on Knox. "Is my father sleeping?"

Knox nods once. "As far as I know."

The sun is cresting on the horizon, painting the sky a pale pink. Back at the manor, the girls will be waking up and preparing for their morning workouts. It stands to reason this is the hour a lot of the shifter city will be waking, and Thorn Tremaine very well may be included in that. But then again, he's the king, making him above all others. He can pretty much do whatever the hell he wants.

"We need to talk." I inch toward Ryne, the rest of the world fading away. "Please."

He flicks his eyes to Knox. "Leave us," he commands, and Knox shuts the door without an ounce of hesitation.

Ryne collapses onto the bottom step and holds his head in his hands.

I sit down on one side of him and Elle on the other. She places a hand on his shoulder, her eyes narrowing. "Why do you trust that human boy so much? Poppy and I should leave."

Ryne shakes his head. "Knox is alright. I know a lot of our kind don't like to let the claimed men get too close, but Knox saved my life when some of my own men failed me."

Elle raises her eyebrows. "How so?"

"I don't want to get into it right now. It's. . . complicated."

Now this is a story I'm dying to hear. I don't think Elle will let that go, but she does. "Are you okay?" she asks at last.

He shakes his head but doesn't look up. "Everything is falling apart. Grady is like a brother to me. I can't kill him, and if we execute Joanna, Poppy's never going to speak to me again."

He reaches out and grips my hand. I study our hands

as my tears swell. His is so large compared to mine, but it fits perfectly. I'm surprised he's willing to display such affection here. It's so public. I should be grateful—I am—but I'm still as torn up as he is about all this. I swallow the angry words I want to say and remain calm. "That's not true. But surely you must see the injustice here. There's no proof that Joanna is in the Resistance. Nor do we even know if there was proof for Nova or Lexi."

But it stands to reason they could've been.

"Don't you see? It doesn't matter. My father can do what he likes, even when it's not right."

Elle lets out a snort. "Careful, Ryne, or your father might think you're in the Resistance as well."

"What is with this resistance movement in the Carolina Pack anyway?" Ryne squeezes my hand tighter. "I know we've had dissent in our past--every pack has--but nothing so organized. Are they really banding together across multiple packs? I'd never even heard of this Resistance group before Anders confessed everything, and no one can adequately explain it to me. I'm supposed to believe everything without proof?"

"It's . . ." I begin, but Elle cuts me off.

"It's a group of women and wolves who want to undermine the current system," she says, matter-of-factly. "Take solace in the fact that this isn't just happening here, Ryne."

"How the hell am I supposed to take solace in that?" he grinds out.

"Because it's all over and in Chicago too. This isn't on you."

"So what have you heard?" He turns on her.

She shrugs. "Just that they don't like the alphas in charge. They want to take over."

"That's not . . ." I start but shut up when Elle gives me a scathing look. But she's wrong. Isn't she? I thought the Resistance wanted to stop the forced mating. It has nothing to do with alphas. At least Joanna never alluded to that. Maybe Elle doesn't know what she's talking about, or maybe she doesn't want Ryne to know too much.

"In Chicago, I was part of a team trying to infiltrate and dismantle the Resistance. It threatens everything your father stands for. Which is why he's so determined to snuff it out here, even if he doesn't have proof that the women Anders targeted are truly part of it."

I still don't know if her words are entirely true or not, but with Elle shooting daggers at me, I don't dare say any more. She and I will have to have a long talk later.

"Why haven't I heard about it until now?" Ryne asks. He looks up, and I expect him to be angry, but he's not. He's shocked and frustrated with himself, as if he never believed he could miss something so big happening right under his nose.

Elle rolls her eyes. "Don't you see, Ryne? Your father

feels threatened by you. You're one of the strongest alphas ever born, and if you were to join such a movement, you might be able to take him down. In fact, there are very few wolves who are aware of its existence or tasked with fighting it. I think Thorn recruited me because I'm no threat since I can't take over."

Ryne tugs me closer to him. "And he trusts Anders?" The disgust in his voice is strong. The fact that Thorn went around Ryne, right to his number two, is pretty low. I imagine this is the kind of thing that would make alphas challenge each other.

Elle stands and stretches, hovering over both of us. "I don't know why he asked Anders to be involved in taking out the resistance. I think he's tried to find one wolf in every pack to root it out in their city. But never the alpha. My guess is Anders was the most ruthless wolf he could think of."

"It should be the alpha," Ryne spits. "This is my pack. Mine."

The door behind us opens, and Ryne jumps up, dropping my hand, every exposed muscle tensing like thick cords of steel. Thorn stands there and then strides down the steps until he's standing a stair above us. He tilts his head. "Is it your pack, Ryne? Because if you ask me, you haven't been acting like a leader in quite some time."

Thorn towers above us with his oily hair slicked back and his fitted button-down shirt and pressed slacks. For all Madame Delphine said about Thorn not being a morning person, he looks as if he's been up for hours. Was Knox lying to us? Or did he simply not know? I really hope Thorn didn't overhear everything.

"Well, what do we have here?" Thorn asks, his eyes roaming over the three of us like he can see every secret written across our skin. Ryne was still holding my hand when Thorn stepped out here. Did he see it? My gut twists because I'm certain he did.

Ryne moves quickly toward Elle and slips his arm around her waist. "Elle often joins me for breakfast. Is that a problem?"

Thorn's eyes land on me.

"Poppy is my best friend," Elle says. "I hate traveling on the boats alone, so she sometimes comes with me because we get so little time to chat just us. She reads in the library while Ryne and I eat." Her voice is smooth as silk, the lie coming out clean.

The king closes the distance between me and him. He runs a thumb along my cheek. "Ah, yes, Poppy, I remember you. Last time I was here, Ryne couldn't keep his eyes off you." He jerks his head back around and chuckles. "Looks like that's still true. You are a pretty little thing, so I can see why. But I can't have you getting in the way of Elle and Ryne's relationship."

"I'm not," I sputter. "Elle's my best friend. I barely even talk to Ryne."

Thorn gives a wicked grin. He thinks this is amusing,

as if I'm a mosquito that needs to be squashed. "I'm not buying that story for a second. So let's fix that, shall we? I haven't taken a wife since Delphine."

"No?" My voice is trembling. I don't even know what I'm doing, except that maybe if I ask enough questions, I can slow this down.

"I've been a single man for eight years. Delphine and I parted ways as soon as Ryne turned fifteen and came of age."

I know Ryne's twenty-three and that Thorn had a number of wives before Madame Delphine. What I don't know is what happened to those other wives. Are they even alive anymore? A knowing chill creeps over me as his eyes narrow on mine.

"I think it's time for a new one. You'll do just fine. After the Pink Moon Festival, you'll return to Chicago with me as my human queen. You'll want for nothing."

Ryne moves for me, but Elle is faster. She inserts herself between me and Thorn, pushing me back. "You can't do that."

Thorn's eyes flash. "Why not? Last I checked, you were not king."

She lets out a breath. "I know. But Nico is her fated. You can't stand between that—it's not our way."

His eyebrows raise. "I admit that I don't really keep up with the drama among Ryne's betas, but I thought I heard that Nico was fated to the woman who died at the Wolf Moon Festival."

Elle shakes her head. "He really liked her. That's why so many people assumed she killed herself. Because he was going to leave her for Poppy."

Thorn clenches his jaw. "I don't appreciate being lied to, Elle." Then he locks eyes on mine. "I don't buy this farce for a second, but even so, I will talk with Nico about this. Something is off about you, dear Poppy, and I'm determined to find out what it is. And when I do, I'm either going to marry you or kill you."

CHAPTER 27

ELLE DOESN'T SAY another word to me until we are on the boat headed home. After Thorn's threat, I thought Ryne was going to challenge him right then and there, but he didn't. We ended up eating breakfast together, and it was a tense affair. Elle managed to keep the conversation flowing, but I don't think I heard a word anyone said. And I still didn't get to talk to Ryne about Joanna. She's going to die, and there is nothing I can do to stop it.

"What was all that about the Resistance?" I accuse Elle, not even bothering to hide my anger.

"Half-truths."

"Why didn't you let me talk?"

She throws her hands in the air. "You can't tell Ryne about them."

"Why not? He actually seems sympathetic."

"That's the problem. He'd understand, but he couldn't safely be a part of it. Oh, he'd want to—I know Ryne well enough to know that. But *Thorn* is his alpha, and he'd never be able to keep this big of a secret from him. Not to mention, that's his own father he'd be working to take down. Do you really think he'd be able to follow through with something like that? It's better to leave Ryne out of it."

Everything she's saying makes it sound like she's part of the Resistance, so if that's the case, her argument doesn't stand. "Isn't Thorn your alpha too?" I challenge. "You're a wolf. How are you keeping these secrets?"

She shuts her mouth and drops her eyes, the blood draining from her face.

"Oh, come on, Elle." My voice goes low. "It's obvious you're involved in this."

She sighs. "Listen, I'm stronger than most people think. They underestimate me, which I use to my advantage. And besides, Thorn hardly questions me on anything. I'm not important enough to him."

"He thinks you're going to marry his son."

"So? I'm a woman. A luna is only special to them because our sons make great alphas. I'm not even ranked. We aren't allowed to be."

I stare at her for a minute, trying to read her sour expression. I know she's probably not allowed to tell me anything, but for whatever reason, I've gotten her to open up just a crack. Time to keep prying. "Will you please tell me if you're a part of the Resistance?" I whisper. We're alone, and the waves lapping against the boat are muffling our conversation, but asking aloud is still terrifying. Doesn't matter—I need to know.

She winks at me. "Are you?"

"I'm not, but I know about it because of Joanna." Time to be brave. "And I want to be."

She grins wickedly and leans back, closing her eyes. The breeze has disappeared since this morning, and the sun is out, and it's as if she's soaking in the rays like a cat. I would join her, but my mind won't slow down.

Something Elle said earlier hits me. "Wait a second, if Ryne can't hide things from Thorn, then how can he hide his feelings for me?"

A ping of insecurity swells through me as her eyes open lazily.

"That's an interesting loophole actually. Because you're Ryne's fated mate, that means he'll do anything to protect you. That counts for this form as well as his wolf form. Thorn knowing about you is a threat to your safety, so Ryne can effectively hide all thoughts about you. It's not easy though. One loving thought or memory of you, and that's it."

"Memory?" I sit up taller. "Tell me how the link works?"

She shrugs. "It's like being part of a shared mind. Thoughts, feelings, memories, images—they all get passed around."

"Do all the packs have this?"

"I don't know about other shifters, but for wolf shifters, yes."

"Does it stay within the pack?"

She hums to herself for a second. "Well, that's tricky. The answer is yes and no. When we travel to another pack, we can't usually access their link without being initiated into the pack. But there are exceptions if the alpha brings you into the link. It's a conscious choice he makes while in wolf form."

"This is getting confusing."

She laughs. "Yeah, Ryne brought me in because he wanted the pack to respect me and see me as important, because we're supposed to get married, but also for my protection since I'm an unmarried woman. But he could just as easily change his mind about that and remove me. If I was initiated though, the only way for me to be removed from the link would be death, exile, or being initiated into a different pack."

"What's the initiation link?"

"If I told you that, I'd have to kill you." Her smile quirks. "It's a sacred ritual—meaning it's a big secret."

"So is that what they mean when they say a wolf comes of age at fifteen? They get initiated into their pack?"

She points at me. "Exactly. And just because Thorn is the alpha over Chicago, don't think he's not linked in when he comes here. He is. There are packs under his command all over the continent, and if any were to show Thorn disrespect, he'd have the alpha replaced immediately."

"And how does Thorn feel about fated mates?"

She blows out a long breath. "Do you want the scary truth or the sugar-coated version?"

"The scary truth."

"The bond toward a fated mate trumps the bond toward anything else, including higher ranks. Since it's considered sacred, and since they're rare, he allows it. But if there were too many fated mates in a pack, I don't doubt he'd feel threatened." Her face goes hard. "And, honey, the Carolina Pack has had three fated matches in a matter of months. Don't think that's gone unnoticed."

I sit back, my mind whirling with everything she explained. It sounds complicated. It also sounds like Ryne is taking huge risks to keep me safe. And as much as I hate it, I finally understand why he's tried to stay away from me and keep our interactions limited. Why he's held off kissing me in the past or stopped more from happening. But I already miss him. I wonder how much longer Ryne and I are going to have to wait. Some days it feels like I've been waiting for him forever, and others like it's only been a moment since we met.

The wedding can't come fast enough. But then that day will be ruined, because my best friend will be executed right before I'm supposed to be married. How can I survive something like that? I force my mind from all these fears and focus back on Elle. As we fly across the river, the spray of the water glistens off her dark cheeks, illuminating her high cheekbones. She's smart, strong, beautiful, and perfect for Ryne. In every way, she's perfect. And part of me wonders if at the end of this, she'll be his mate after all.

"There's got to be something we can do," I say to Abi, my voice hollow. We're lying in our beds, staring up at the dark ceiling. Outside, the moon is only two days away from waxing full, and we're not any closer to saving Joanna and Grady. I'm more determined than ever to join the Resistance, but with Joanna gone and Elle keeping her mouth shut, I can't figure out who to even talk to. Abi has been right by my side, wanting to help too, and feeling just as frustrated. I've told her some of what's happened with Ryne but not everything. I'm still keeping the secret about the weddings.

After that fateful morning where King Thorn caught Ryne holding my hand, Thorn sent word that Elle was to leave Drayton Hall and officially move in with Ryne. We haven't seen her since, and Faye keeps telling everyone it's because she's on a pre-honeymoon with Ryne. I've wanted to slap her for it, to put her in her place and tell her that Ryne loves *me*, but what can I do? I'm sworn to secrecy. And besides, we haven't seen him either. Her assumption makes sense from the outside looking in.

Abi sighs. "What about your dress fitting today? Was there anyone there that seemed like they could be part of the Resistance?"

"No," I reply miserably. "I'd hoped Elle would've been there, but she wasn't. And when I tried to talk with the seamstress about Joanna, she poked me and told me to mind my manners." The dress fitting had been a horrible experience anyway. None of the choices were close to anything I'd like to get married in, so I ended up letting the workers choose for me.

"That's it," I say, jumping from the bed. "I'm going to Madame Delphine."

At this point, I'm beyond caring who knows I want to be part of the Resistance. I'll do anything to save Joanna. There is no way I'm letting Ryne execute her. Elle said he'd do anything to protect me. Maybe I'll put myself between him and Joanna.

"I'm coming with you," Abi squeaks, and together we pad from our bedroom and down the dark hallway. The girls are supposed to be sleeping, but with the festival coming up, I doubt very many of them are. Last thing I need is for one of them to catch me out here and try to use it against me somehow.

We reach Madame Delphine's door, and I tap on it. No answer. I tap a little louder and hear her murmur from inside.

"Crap. I think you woke her up," Abi hisses.

"What's going on?" Madame Delphine peeks her head through the door and stares up at me. I'm tall, so I'm used to women looking up at me, but when she does it, it makes me feel like when Mama used to chastise me. "Are you okay?"

"May we please come in?" I ask. I don't want to answer her questions here.

She considers it for a moment and then widens the door to let us through. Her room is warm and cozy, with a big bed and rumpled blankets from where she'd clearly been sleeping. "On with it," she says. "Although I suspect I already know what this is about." Her face is irritated, but her eyes are sympathetic. "Again."

"Joanna," I confirm, trying to keep the tremble out of my voice.

She gives me a sad frown. "There's nothing I can do for the girl."

But I heard her with Elle. I know she cares about Joanna. I know she thinks Thorn is a tyrant. And if Elle is part of the Resistance, then it stands to reason Madame Delphine could be as well.

Time to gather my courage and ask.

"Are you in the Resistance?" Abi beats me to it. "Because we're pretty sure you are."

My lips twitch a little. I didn't know Abi had it in her to be so bold. It was a very Joanna-like move. But then I shouldn't be surprised, since Joanna's influence has rubbed off on us.

Madame Delphine's weary eyes grow alert and narrow. "How dare you speak of such things." Her words come out in a hiss. But she doesn't deny it. And she doesn't even sound that mad.

I inch closer to her, eager now. "You are, aren't you?"

She sputters and shifts back a few steps. I've never seen her so flustered. "Of course I'm not. Why would I be part of an organization that goes against my son?"

Abi isn't buying it, and neither am I.

"Maybe because you want to help him." I stand a little taller. "Maybe because you know first-hand, better than anybody, how dangerous Thorn is, and if someone doesn't stand up to him, eventually he's going to kill Ryne."

"Get out," she snaps.

I don't expect it, and it feels like a slap.

"But we want to help," Abi protests.

I nod. "I have an idea. One that could save Joanna."

"No." Madame Delphine's tone is hard. "I am not part of the Resistance, and you are not either. Whatever this plan is, it's foolish and dangerous and must be forgotten immediately. Joanna will die, and there is nothing you can do to stop it. It will hurt, and you will move on. You must remember your place, else you end up like her."

She ushers us to the door and into the hallway.

"But if you'd be willing to hear me out, I think—"

"Enough!" She slams the door in my face.

I turn to Abi.

"What are we going to do now?" she asks.

"We're going to save her ourselves. Are you prepared for something like that?"

Her mouth thins into a determined line. "I have nothing left to lose."

CHAPTER 28

THE MORNING OF THE FESTIVAL, I wake with my stomach in knots. I peer over at Abi to find her eyes wide open as well. It's early, but the showers are already going. Tonight, two new betas are going to be introduced to the remaining claimed girls, and they want to look their best.

Tonight, Abi goes to the mating house.

Tonight, we're going to save my best friend.

Or die trying.

I roll over and face Abi. "Are you ready?" I ask.

She shakes her head. "No. But I have to be."

"We got this." Dinner from the night before threatens to come up, but I swallow it down. I can't show Abi that I'm scared. Her part in the plan is crucial.

The morning passes excruciatingly slow, but at the same time speeds by. I can't figure out how that is possible. We don't have afternoon classes because we all have to get ready for the festival.

I grab Abi's hand and head to the stairs, but before we can go up to our room, Madame Delphine stops us.

"You're getting ready in the city," she says to me.

"What? Why?" I sputter.

"Because you are marrying Nico tonight, or did you forget that?"

"I didn't forget. I just had other things on my mind. Like my best friend getting executed for no reason."

"I understand." She nods. "But brides go into the city. Abi will come over with the rest of us."

Abi shoots me a panicked look. I squeeze her hand. This wasn't part of the plan, but we'll have to roll with it. "Harlow and Katelyn will help you get ready. You'll be okay." I turn to Madame Delphine. "Alright, let's do this."

She tilts her head. "The beta wives have your wedding dress ready to go, and they'll be helping you get ready. Are you prepared to behave?"

"Why wouldn't I behave?"

She doesn't answer that. Instead she says, "It's very important that you get along with them. These women will be your peers from here out."

I swallow and think of saving Joanna instead of these women I'm supposed to impress. My plan would work so much better if I had a dress I could easily move in, but the tailor saw to it that my poofy monstrosity is skintight through the bodice, and it has about a million pounds in the skirt. Too bad it may have to get torn in the process. I don't care—this plan has to work. Joanna's life depends on it.

And then once she's saved, Ryne and I will get married.

A car is waiting for me, but it's not Knox behind the wheel. I've never seen this guy before. He doesn't say a word to me as we drive into the city. That's probably for the best. He pulls up to a large white house with towering columns and round porches. Another car has just pulled up behind us. Elle gets out and gives me a nod but doesn't say anything. She's wearing white silky-looking pajamas, and her hair looks freshly braided. It feels like I haven't seen her in ages, and I want to ask her a million things all at once.

We climb the stairs together. "Where have you been?" I ask.

She shakes her head. "Not now."

We knock on the door, and a stout woman answers, squealing. There are about thirty women all laughing behind her. The woman pulls us into the room and slips elegant glasses filled with pink champagne into our hands.

She claps. "Oh, this is so exciting. Usually we don't get to do this except for the wedding season right after the Harvest Moon Festival. Ladies, by the time we are done with you, you won't recognize yourselves."

Elle and I are ushered off to different rooms. I am plucked and waxed, and it takes hours to do my makeup, hair, and nails. When they try to make my nails longer, I refuse. I already feel like I don't belong in my own body. I have to keep something normal.

I'm taken to another room, which has my huge white dress slung over the couch. Two women help me into it. It's corseted and pushes my breasts up, but even then, I don't have much cleavage. They tie the strings tight, and I can hardly breathe. Sleeves that fall off my shoulders reveal a peekaboo of skin, and the skirt poofs out like a gigantic cupcake. I swear it sticks out six feet in all directions. There is no way in hell that I'm going to be able to move in this thing, but I'm just going to have to suck it up and force it.

I nearly get stuck in the doorway on the way out, but I somehow make it down the stairs into the main room without falling onto my face. Elle stands in the entryway in a sleek cream wedding gown that looks fantastic on her. There is a slit that practically goes up to her hip, and I'm jealous because if she needs to run, she can. Why didn't they offer a dress like that for me?

Her lips twitch when she spots me.

"Nice dress," she says with a sly smile. "You look like a princess."

"Thanks," I grumble. "Maybe we should switch."

"Not happening." She nudges me and drops her lips

to my ear. "Our plan is still on. Try to be happy about that."

I jerk away from her. As much as I love Ryne, I can't think about that right now. When she says "plan," all I can think of is the one with Abi, but I know she's talking about marrying Ryne. "I'm not going to be happy until Joanna is safe and sound. If he kills her, there is no way I'm going through with any wedding. How could I?"

The chatter in the room suddenly dies down. Elle chuckles, but her eyes are hard. "Ignore her. She just hates getting dressed up and is nervous about the wedding. Come on, Poppy, our carriage awaits."

She motions toward the door.

I swallow.

It's time.

After tonight, nothing will be the same. I'll either rescue my best friend or die in this horrendous dress.

It's late March, so spring is in full bloom when we arrive at the venue. I expect to be taken to one of the old city buildings or at least be getting married inside, but we're not. We're back at the very same park where I watched Ryne kill all those wolves who challenged him, the one across from his stately home. Back then, it had been cold and dreary, but today the park has been entirely transformed. My mouth falls open, and a little purr of approval comes out, despite my better judgment.

"Tell me about it," Elle says. And then we're being ushered from the safety of the town car. The other patrons haven't arrived yet, so I'm able to take it all in without distraction. The trees are flowering with buds of pink and white, tulips line the walkways, and pansies in every shade crowd the flower beds. And in the middle of it all, a series of crisp white tents have been erected. At least, I think they're tents. I'm not really sure what they are because they're so grand and pretty. They're open on all sides and big enough to fit a hundred people in each. I've never seen anything like it. At the end of the tents, out in the open field, a stage has been built. I've seen enough stages in my time here that I know it can't be good. That's probably where they're going to kill Joanna and Grady—I force myself to look away.

A waft of savory food tickles my nose, and my stomach growls. I haven't eaten in hours, and I'm used to eating three solid meals a day now. I've gained at least ten pounds of much-needed weight since arriving here. I frown, because how many times had I gone to bed hungry as a kid? And how many villagers live on the barest scraps while the shifters live in luxury?

And okay, not all the wolves live in luxury, but if I end up marrying Ryne today—or even Nico—then I will. I've been so blinded by my feelings for Ryne that

I've forgotten to ask myself this one very important question: how am I going to live with myself?

How am I going to live with myself if Joanna dies?

If humans continue to be treated like slaves?

If the girls keep getting sent to the mating houses?

If Anders gets away with killing so many innocent women?

If the king continues to rule over Ryne, and Ryne continues to take it?

"No," I snap.

"What?" Elle asks. I hadn't meant to say the words out loud. She stares, and from the knowing look she gives me, I wonder if she's thinking the same questions. Maybe they've been haunting her much longer than they've been haunting me. It's no wonder she's in the Resistance. Even though she won't admit it aloud, I know it's true. I won't be able to make it much longer here without joining myself. I can't sit around and do nothing anymore.

"Nothing," I reply, and it physically hurts me to say it.

But she knows better, knows I'm a liar and that nothing is most definitely something. And I can only hope that when the time comes, she'll be on my side.

CHAPTER 29

I STARE out from the little plastic window of the small tent that Elle and I are taken to and told is the bridal room. We've been swarmed with the same hair and makeup crew who are applying the final touches. "Let's fix your lipstick," one says to me, her voice pleased with herself and excited. I couldn't care less. I relax and open my lips, but I don't look at her as she glides something thick and gooey across them. My eyes are still trained on the window.

I don't care about the newcomers, the beta families all dressed up, or even our claimed girls who come prancing down the sidewalks like a row of colorful spring flowers in their special pastel Pink Moon Festival dresses. The arriving guests only keep my attention for a short moment, long enough to see if it's who I'm waiting for.

Joanna.

I don't want to miss her.

I have to help her. And I hate to think about it, but if my plan fails, I have to at least say goodbye.

My eyes start to water.

"Oh, none of that," the makeup girl chastises. "This is your special day!"

"She's just really happy," Elle lies for me.

Our eyes meet, and she nods once in understanding. She's as worried as I am. Maybe I'm not so alone. I reach out and grab her hand, and she squeezes back in solidarity. I'm reminded of how much she's risking with this too. If things go south, her family could end up dead.

"Are you ready for this?" she asks.

No.

"Yes," I lie.

I gaze back out the window to see Shauna and Amos. They look happy, which makes me a touch happier too. I wish I could've spent another evening with them, laughing around Shauna's dinner table and talking about flowers. After the engagement to Nico was announced, Justin backed off completely. We didn't even talk about it. All I got was an understanding nod from him, and that was the end of our relationship. It was time to move on.

"Look!" Elle jumps up, and her hair and makeup people scatter in protest. "That's my family. My mom and dad and my four brothers."

Sure enough, a beautiful family strolls down the sidewalk. Her mother looks so much like her, ebony-skinned and petite and absolutely beautiful. She's an aging human with some gray in her hair and wrinkles around her mouth and eyes. Her appearance is a good twenty years older than her fit-looking husband, but the man holds to her arm like he doesn't mind it at all, like he'll be proud to stay with her until her dying day, and may even stay single thereafter.

It makes me smile.

Elle's father is perhaps the largest shifter man I've ever seen. His head is shaved and shiny, which is different from the shifters I've seen who keep their hair long. Her brothers look to be both older and younger than her, but all close in age. They're copies of their handsome father but with jet-black curly hair. The boys catch the gazes of many of the men and women as they find their places among the waiting crowd below the stage. How could they not? They're gorgeous, and from the looks of it, single.

Off on a distant lawn, little white chairs are set up in rows facing an arbor decorated in white roses and shiny gold ribbons. Madame Delphine made me practice the ceremony back at the manor a couple of times this week, but it's not much different than the ones the humans use. Soon I'll be standing under that arc, proclaiming my love and sealing my fate. The question still remains as to who.

A thought strikes me—when will Ryne find the time to initiate Elle and her family into the pack? Has he already done it? He would do it before the ceremony. So maybe he already has?

No.

Because the other wolves arriving would question why they suddenly have eight new pack members. I still don't know what the initiation is, but it can't be simple. Nothing about these wolves is simple. I grimace to myself—this isn't going to be easy to pull off. Especially not with King Thorn overseeing it all. With that final thought, the last to arrive are the grooms and the king himself. They climb out of the same car. King Thorn first, then Ryne, then Nico.

My breath catches, snagging somewhere between my heart and my head. I don't know what to do about Ryne, and I don't think he'll forgive me, but I'll never forgive myself if I don't go through with this. I can only hope that when it's over, he'll still want me as his wife.

The sun begins to set, and lights brighten the field and twinkle among the trees. The warmth of the spring day lingers, mixing with the sweet scent of all the fresh flowers. The tent flap opens, and a woman sticks her head in. "It's time," she says. She's holding two massive flower bouquets. She hands the white calla lilies to Elle and the crimson poppies to me. I take them eagerly, wondering if these were chosen from the ones I grew. I know it seems silly, but I decide that they are, and that makes me feel a little bit better.

The weddings won't be first. Starting with the gore and ending with the celebration seems to be the wolf way, and as we step out into the blinding sunset, I realize we're wanted out here for display, as if to say, "Look at our lovely brides" and "This is the prize betas earn when they stay in line."

All the other claimed girls are already next to the stage, preening and waving to the betas milling about. There are no chairs for us. Not that I'd be able to sit in this monster of a dress anyway. Ryne is talking to his father across the stage as Elle and I walk up the stairs. He lifts his gaze and meets my eye. The connection is undeniable. I couldn't break it even if I wanted to, and I don't want to.

"Stop staring at him," Elle hisses in my ear. I tear my eyes away from his, and Elle blows Ryne a kiss. Thorn's mouth presses into a straight line. I wonder if he noticed. Hopefully he thought Ryne was staring at Elle. He'd probably be unhappy to see me no matter who I was looking at; the man has it out for me. Which makes it all the more terrifying that he tried to make me his wife. Unless he was bluffing. If he knows the truth about me, I'm doomed.

We take our positions in front of the other girls, and several of them glare at me. Abi moves to stand right behind me and grips my hand, passing me the dagger that is supposed to be tucked safely under my pillow back at the manor. We'd planned to take care of this part back at Drayton Hall before Madame Delphine had taken me away. Nobody seems to notice as I adjust the blade so it's hidden between my hands and the massive bouquet of poppies. It's part of a matching set, and Abi has the other one hidden in her bodice.

I look around at the crowd. It's mostly betas and their wives, all dressed up, standing in front of the stage. But beyond the park, swarming the streets, are the gammas and the deltas. The park is surrounded by wolves on all sides, most in their human forms, but some have shifted. I should be used to it by now, but it still makes me nervous every time I see one of them in their wolf form. They can inflict so much damage with claws and teeth.

Even if I do manage to save Joanna and Grady, the odds that they make it out alive are slim to none. Those wolves will tear me apart if their alpha commands it. They'd be more than happy to. And for the first time, I wonder if Thorn can command them, or if orders like that have to come directly from Ryne. I'm afraid I won't like the answer to that question, but I have to do something about Joanna and Grady. I can't let Ryne execute them.

I can't.

Once we are in position, Thorn takes his place at the center of the stage.

"Friends and family, tonight's festival won't only be the usual releasing of the lowest-ranked claimed women into the mating houses. Tonight, we have not one, but two special events planned. My son has chosen a bride, and he will wed her at the end of the evening, but first, we are to have a public execution of some very dangerous and equally foolish criminals. They are traitors and do not deserve to live."

A roar goes up among the crowd, and my stomach sours. King Thorn waits for them to quiet down with a smug expression on his face. He motions for one of his men to come forward. The man hands him a long sword. Thorn takes it and swishes it about a few times with that wicked grin he so often carries.

"Beheading is appropriate, is it not?"

Once again the crowd shouts their approval.

"As much as I like a good beheading, this is not my territory. The honor belongs to my son." He holds the sword out to Ryne, who takes it easily, as if he's used it before. I think I'm going to be sick.

"Bring in the prisoners," Thorn cries. He and Ryne take a step back. I crane my neck around to see. A path has formed in the street behind the stage. Several men carry a board about two feet wide and eight feet long on their shoulders. On top of the board are two people sitting back to back. My heart tightens. Joanna looks like she's been roughed up, and her eyes are blindfolded, her mouth gagged, and her hands and feet are both bound with tight cords. A rope ties her to Grady.

The men on either side of the path spit on her and Grady as they pass. One loogie hits her right in the cheek. I clench my fists. She doesn't deserve this. Neither of them does.

The men set the board down on the stage, and I can see that Joanna is trembling. Grady fights against his binds, but they are tied tight. I wonder why he can't shift and get away, but there must be something to the binding preventing it. I try to get a closer look, but he's moving so much it's hard to see. If I'm going to save either of them, I have to start with him. I've seen his wolf—I know he can fight.

Ryne steps forward, and Abi leans into me. "Now."

She launches herself across the stage with me on her heels. I can't move like I want to, but I can't think about that right now. I accidentally drop my flowers, and some of the poppies scatter across the stage. But I've still got a hold of the dagger—I cling to it like a lifeline.

Ryne glances up at us, and Abi throws herself at him, the sword falling from his hand.

"Save me from the mating house," she yells. Her mouth puckers, as if trying to kiss him, and several people in the crowd laugh. They know a kiss from the alpha could save her and are roaring at her expense.

I reach Joanna and Grady, crouching down between them and Thorn so he cannot see what is happening.

My dress is good for that at least. I have no idea what's going on behind me, but at any moment someone could grab me and pull me off. The blade is sharp and slides easily through the rope on Grady's hands. I cut the rope to his feet and the one that binds him to Joanna. By now, he's ripped off his blindfold and spit out his gag.

"Thank you," he whispers as I move to Joanna.

Hands grab my shoulders, and I'm flying backward, losing my grip on the knife. I hit the stage, and my head cracks on the hardwood. Stars flash in my eyes as I sit up. I cannot afford to waste any time, nor do I know who attacked me.

I look back over at Joanna, but I'm distracted when Ryne tackles Grady, both of them tumbling off the stage. Did Ryne throw me off? Anger burns at that realization, and I scramble to right myself. Thorn is watching everything unfold intently, as is the rest of the crowd, including the betas on stage, *including* Nico. They're all a bunch of cowards. I quickly crawl back over to Joanna, but now that I have no blade, this will be much harder.

She is bucking and thrashing, trying to get free of her bindings.

"It's me," I say to her. "Calm down and let me get these off of you."

She stills, and I go to work on the ropes binding her hands. Abi crouches next to me and starts on the ones at her feet.

Elle comes up and helps me with the hands. "If

anyone asks, I was trying to stop you," she whispers. I could hug her right now, but there's no time. People can see us, but I doubt they can tell what's really going on.

We manage to get Joanna's hands undone, and she rips off her blindfold and gag.

She coughs and looks around frantically with blood-shot eyes. "Where's Grady?"

"That doesn't matter. You need to run," I say, pulling her up and shoving her toward the other girls.

"I'm going with you," Abi says.

"I'm not leaving without him." Joanna clenches her fists and cranes her neck around to see over my shoulder.

"No," she cries and shoves past me.

Her cry is swallowed by Grady's soul-crushing wail. It's so deep and painful and awful that tears instantly blur my eyes. I smell the blood before I see it.

CHAPTER 30

It's my first thought. I wonder why they didn't shift. When Ryne killed before, he shifted first. The wolves would snarl and bite and claw as wolves do. But this time, they stayed humans, and he went for Grady with that damned sword. Grady had no way to protect himself. And maybe that was the point. Maybe Grady wasn't allowed the dignity of dying in his truest form.

The cheers grow to deafening heights, and I can no longer hear any screams as I force myself to take the whole scene in.

Grady lies in the grass, and a few feet away from him, his right arm claws outward toward the stage. A line of red connects the arm to the body. My stomach twists.

Joanna runs for him, and miraculously, he sits up.

So he's not dead. Not yet, anyway.

He looks around with wide shocked eyes and then to his severed limb. He's losing so much blood and fast. Joanna falls to her knees at his side and grabs a hold of what's left of his bleeding arm. Then she goes for his pants, attempting to undo his belt with trembling fingers. The crowd of wolves from the streets has surged into the park, forming a tight half-circle around Grady and Joanna. Most are dressed in t-shirts and jeans, but a few wear hooded shirts, casting their faces in darkness.

"Leave her!" Thorn bellows. The crowd quiets, and he continues. "Let her try to save him. This should be fun."

The crowd laughs and watches gleefully as she attempts to cut off the flow of blood by cinching the belt around what's left of his bloody stump.

I run toward them. I have to help.

Arms grab me and hold me back. "Stop, Poppy. You can't." It's Nico's voice of reason in my ear, and suddenly, I hate him.

"Let me go!" I scream, my voice growing hoarse. I squirm and drop my weight, but it's no use. His hold is iron tight.

"If you go over there, Ryne will be forced to kill you too," Nico hisses in my ear. "Joanna wouldn't want that. Nobody would want that."

I stomp on his foot, not bothering to inform him that Ryne would never kill me.

"I'm bored," Thorn calls out. "And the moon is

coming. Son, it's time to end this and begin the festivities."

Ryne swings his sword around, which the crowd loves even more. It shines silver and bloodied under the lights. Sometime during all that, the sun has disappeared, and the full moon rises. It's not a white or yellow moon, but rather, it's a brutal shade of red—a rare blood moon. My mama always said blood moons were a bad omen, that they brought death and destruction with them. I've only seen a few in my lifetime, and they always gave me a sense of bad things to come.

How fitting that we'd get one tonight of all nights.

I stomp on Nico's foot again, and he drops me with a curse. Then I scramble away and crawl toward my friends. Nico goes for the hem of my skirts, calling for me to wait, but I kick him again and continue forward.

"What's this?" The king laughs as I practically tumble off the stage, but his voice is filled with malice. "Has another come to die?"

My skin buzzes. My ears too. I don't allow fear to come in. I keep my eyes on Joanna and Grady. Nobody else. Not even Ryne.

I leap for them, land in a crouch, and raise my head, looking into the fuming ocean blue of Ryne's eyes.

"If you are going to kill them, you'll have to kill me first." My words come out breathy and weak.

Ryne narrows his eyes. "Step aside, Poppy," he

growls, only for me to hear. "I have no choice." And then he adds louder, "I am the alpha!"

I stand up, and even though I'm still several inches shorter than him, I feel invincible. I take a step toward him, and the crowd moves closer in on us. I can practically feel them at my back. I want to shout at them to move away and not to hurt Grady, but I keep my eyes on Ryne.

"Then you'll have to kill me."

"Poppy." His low voice comes out in a strangled cry. "Don't do this."

"Kill her, son." Thorn's ugly voice slices through the crowd. "Do as she asks."

"Poppy," Ryne whispers my name, and in that moment I know I've just broken his heart. And by forcing him to put me before the pack, I'm breaking my own heart too.

But it has to be done.

"You can't, can you?" I shout my answer. "Because we're fated. You can't deny it anymore. You can't kill me because you love me, and our bond is stronger than even the call of your alpha." I look over Ryne's shoulder. Thorn's mouth is pressed into a straight line. I always knew he hated me, and now I've let everyone know why.

A hush falls over the crowd, and no one moves.

"Is this true?" Thorn asks. He steps closer as if he's shocked by this revelation. Of course that is another one of his manipulations.

Ryne hangs his head for a moment and drops the sword. He turns and faces his father.

"Yes, Father, it's true. Poppy is my fated mate. I cannot deny it."

Thorn is quiet for a very long time, and then he begins to laugh. It's a quiet laugh at first, just a snort, but within seconds, he's doubled over, roaring with laughter.

He must be mad.

I take advantage of the distraction and turn around. I come face-to-face with a large shirtless man. He's bald but has bulky muscles and smells strongly of body odor. He leers at me. "Looking for a real man, kitten? How dare you embarrass our alpha."

I take a step back and try to spot Joanna and Grady, but the crowd around me and Ryne is too thick. Everyone is pressed in, and there isn't a sign of either of them except blood on the ground.

My plan worked.

Joanna and Grady are gone.

And no one seems to notice that they've disappeared. Every eye is on me and Ryne. Thorn recovers from his outburst and stands tall, adjusting his tie. Behind him, Nico stares at me, his eyes unbelieving. I can't tell if the expression is one of sorrow or relief. He never loved me, this much I know.

"I'm disappointed in you, Ryne," Thorn says coolly. "For years I tried to have an heir. Several women failed me until I found your mother, and then she only gave me you. One child. One son who's so weak that he cannot put a woman in her place." His eyes land on me. "It disgusts me."

Thorn is circling the area, and without a moment's notice, he reaches out and grabs Elle by the arm, tugging her close to him. She cries out.

"I promised a wedding tonight, and a wedding we'll get. Ryne has been a weak alpha and will need to prove himself to me again. Is he worthy of a luna after this pathetic display? I think not!" he bellows. The crowd grows agitated. Ryne is their alpha, and it's as if they don't know how to take any of this. "Anders, come!" Anders rushes to Thorn's side. "Challenge Ryne. It's time for a new alpha of the Carolina Pack. And when you are alpha, then you can wed Elle."

Anders's face pales. He knows he cannot win. "That's . . . that's your son."

Thorn shrugs. "I like you better."

Anders is still shocked, but something bright in his eyes indicates that he's thought of this many times before. How long has he waited to be the alpha? I shiver to think what would happen to this pack if Anders were in charge.

So far, Ryne hasn't moved an inch. His body is taught like steel wires. I want to reach out and grab his hand, but I know that would be foolish. He keeps himself between me and his father so that I cannot be hurt, but I desperately want to see his face. I want him to know that I'm with him, that I love him, that I'm his... but he doesn't look at me.

Anders stares at him, not saying a single word.

Then without warning, he changes into his large brown wolf and leaps at Ryne.

Ryne reaches back and shoves me into the crowd seconds before shifting into his wolf. If I were smart, I'd run, but I can't leave Ryne. We are connected. If he dies, I'll die, because I can't imagine going on without him.

I can't...

CHAPTER 31

THEY CIRCLE each other for a moment, and the men around me jostle forward, blocking my view. I shove at hard flesh, but no one is letting me through. Snarls and thuds come from where they are fighting, but I still can't see. I drop to the ground and try to crawl forward, but my blasted dress is stuck under someone's boot.

"Stop!" Anders's voice rings out. "I don't want to do this!"

"So you concede?" Thorn replies. "So soon? What happened to the man that hunted down Resistance members so mercilessly? And now you concede after barely a minute of brawling with my pathetic son?"

I wish I could see what's going on. I tug on my dress.

"I do not wish to kill Ryne," Anders says. More like he doesn't want to die. He knows how strong Ryne is and has seen countless wolves die trying to usurp him.

He's smart to refuse, but I still saw that look in his eyes. He'd do it if he knew he could win.

"Then you will be exiled," Thorn growls. "That's the price of conceding."

"Stop, Father," Ryne yells. "You've made your point. But this is my pack, and you need to stand down."

I manage to get to my feet, and they all come back into view. I'm surrounded by wolf shifters that I've never met before, and one of them grabs my wrist, but I shake him off and shove my way to the front.

"What are you going to do, Ryne?" Thorn growls. "Are you going to marry that pathetic human mate or the powerful luna I've been saving for you?"

Everyone turns to Ryne then. We all want to know.

Me the most.

The moon shines down on us, blood red lighting the planes of Ryne's face. But before he can answer, wolves begin to howl.

Not wolves—lycans.

I jerk my head around to find they're all around us, mixed into the crowd, towering on their haunches and growling with thirst. They must have come as humans, planting themselves here before the moon fully rose and took over their infected bodies. I'd always thought of the lycans as bloodthirsty creatures with no control over their actions, but here they are, organized and ready to fight. To be able to pull off something like this means they must have far more control over their human forms than I thought. My mind spins with the implications. What does it all mean?

That thought gets cut off as one of them jumps, flying over the men and women, coming directly toward me. I can see death in its red eyes. It wants to take me out. Announcing my relationship to Ryne in front of this crowd meant announcing it to the lycanthrope.

Ryne spots me, grabs my wrist, and pulls me out from the crowd. A second later, the lycan lands where I was standing and screeches out a desperate howl. With one swoop, Ryne hoists me up into his arms and leaps back up on the stage where the betas are circling the girls to protect them. He sets me down in the middle, shoves me next to Abi, and shifts back into his wolf form without a word.

All around me the men have shifted into wolves or lycan.

All of them but one.

Thorn still stands in the middle of the stage—a lone man.

His angry eyes meet mine, and I raise my head in defiance. Three lycan jump up onto the stage behind him, and I hope they tear him to shreds. But before they can reach him, he rushes for me, knocking over the betas. He wraps a strong arm around my waist and pulls me out from their protection. He spins me around and shoves me right at the three lycan.

The monster's sharp claws scratch at my arms and

sides. It burns, and I scream out. That only seems to encourage them. One grabs a hold of my cupcake skirt, and it tears away from my dress, leaving me standing in a thin white slip. I can't fight them—I have no weapons. I drop to the ground and scramble to the edge of the stage, a trail of blood behind me from the claws that tore open my skin. Two shifter wolves have joined the fray. I spot Ryne a few feet from the stage battling a lycan.

I want to cry out for him, but I don't want him to get distracted.

Pain shoots up my leg, pain that burns like liquid fire. I cry out and glance back in time to see a silver wolf clamp its jaws down on the lycan that's mere inches from me. I tumble off the stage and run.

It's slow going at first. I limp from the fire in my leg, and fights are raging all over the park, but I weave my way to the edge of the fighting crowd, leaving the rest of the claimed girls on the stage.

Everyone is focused on killing each other and none seem to notice me. I have no idea where to go. Behind me is the park, and in front of me is the inky black river. It's high with the spring runoff from the mountains up north. There's no way I can safely try to cross it.

I let out a frightened cry and run toward the houses instead. I'm not really sure where I'm going, just away. I manage to pass several homes and then realize I've rounded the park, and I'm right in front of Ryne's house. This is probably not a safe place to be. Ryne is obviously a target of the lycans, but merely the sight of his home makes me want to sob with relief.

A voice calls out my name behind me, and I nearly falter. It's not the voice I want to hear, but it's a welcome one.

I slow and turn around.

"Knox," I breathe, and soon he's right in front of me.

"What happened?" he asks, his eyes searching my body for wounds. His mouth is pulled tight in worry and sweat beads along his hairline.

"I don't know," I reply. "It all happened so fast."

"You're bleeding," he says, dropping down to examine my leg. He tears off a part of his shirt and wraps it around the wound. "Come on, let's get you inside."

"No," I say a little too forcefully. "Thorn knows about me and Ryne. He'll kill me if he finds me in there."

Knox stares at me for a moment, and suddenly I wish none of this had ever happened. That Knox had not been claimed and that Willow had never died. Then we'd probably be married by now, living a peaceful life back home among the fields. And not here, not trapped in a wolf shifter war, not slaves to a broken system, not targets for crazed lycans.

But then I never would've met Ryne.

And it's true that I never did have Ryne, but I had his kisses, and I had the dream of him, the hope of us—and if I'm being honest, that means more to me than a million lifetimes with Knox ever could have.

Knox gives a short nod. "Then come with me. We'll get you in the car and wait for Ryne. He'll know what to do."

But he won't.

Because I can already feel the virus moving through me, a liquid fire thickening in my veins like a death sentence, circling right back to the pain in my leg, demanding I acknowledge the truth.

I've been bitten by a lycan.

CHAPTER 32

I STARE out of the window of the car and try not to cry. Knox hasn't moved the car, but he waits, leaning against the outside. He doesn't have any weapons, and I don't understand how he can be so calm. After what seems like hours, I spot Ryne striding across the grass. He looks uninjured, but his head hangs low.

Knox calls out for him, and he comes running. I can't hear what they're saying, but Knox hands him a pair of pants. He jerks them on and then yanks the car door open.

Relief floods his features as he catches sight of me. "You're alive."

"I am." But I can't find any joy in the statement.

He slides in next to me and wraps me into a hug. I try not to cry on his shoulder. Knox closes the door behind him, and within seconds the car is flying down the road.

"Are the lycans gone?" I ask.

He nods once. "Not before they took a bunch of us out. I'm pretty sure my father was their target."

I hate that I hope Thorn is dead. But I do. "And is he—"

"He's alive." His voice is sharp. "But we lost Cade. And a couple other betas. Most of those who died were my deltas and gammas. They died to protect me."

I can hear the hatred in his voice. I hope he isn't directing it at himself. The lycans organized this. They planned this. Ryne's pack was simply doing what they were born to do—defend their alpha.

We ride in silence for a while, and my aching leg starts to go numb.

"Where are we going?" I ask. My voice is shaking now. I know what I have to confess, but the words are caught in my throat.

"Away from the city where we can regroup. I don't know what's going to happen with my father and Elle and her family now. But the secret is out. You made sure of that." He chuckles for a moment. I thought he'd be mad. He pulls away and stares at me straight in the eyes. I can't help the tears that stream down my face.

He cups my cheeks and wipes at the wetness with his thumb. "Come on, Poppy, don't cry. We'll figure it out. We're together now, and that's all that matters."

"We can't be together."

"Of course we can. My father tried to have me replaced back there. He failed, and now I will never let him get between you and me ever again."

It's everything I've wanted to hear, but it's too late. I make myself stop crying, gathering my strength as I pull away from him and lift my foot into his lap.

"We can't be together because I've been bitten by a lycan. Please kill me quickly. I don't want it to hurt."

Ryne freezes. He doesn't say anything for a long moment. He just stares at the wrapped wound, a haunted sheen over his face and pain in his eyes.

"Are . . . are you sure?"

I've never heard him sound so broken, and it shatters me. "Look for yourself."

He gently unwraps the cloth and runs his fingers along the bite mark. There's no denying what it is. I shouldn't turn until the next full moon, but it doesn't matter. It's already a death sentence. I know how this works. We both do.

"Knox," he calls out in a strangled voice. "Drive us to the wilds' edge."

Then he pulls me close and holds me tight.

We stay like that for a while. As my mind clears, my eyes focus on the night outside. We're driving away from the city, and the houses grow farther and farther apart. If there are electric lights in these houses, they must be off or not working because they're all dark. More likely the homes are abandoned because they are so close to the wilds. I assume Ryne's having Knox take me away so he can kill me in private, allowing me some semblance of dignity in the act.

But then again, why take me away from the city for that?

He's not going to kill me.

I sit up, peeling myself off of him.

"Are you sure?" I ask, and he knows what I mean because he immediately nods. "Isn't that against wolf law or something?" I ask.

He shushes me seconds before his hands cup my face, and he brings my mouth to his. I don't care that Knox is here. My thoughts melt away with Ryne's kiss. And my heart aches.

I'm losing him.

We're losing each other.

And this is our goodbye, not spoken with our voices, but spoken with our lips.

I'm not ready for it to be over when he pulls away because the car has come to a stop. We climb out, and I wince when my foot hits the pavement. I can't help it; the pain is throbbing. Ryne winces too, but his face is unreadable in the darkness. Maybe that's a good thing. I'm in nothing but a slip and corseted bodice. My feet are bare. I lost my high heels ages ago. I have nothing left.

My eyes start to adjust to the moon, and I long to

look at it, as if the moon and I already have a deal together, as if we've already signed the agreement in blood. I force myself to take in my surroundings instead. There's no bridge and no river—not like when I first came into the shifter city. In fact, the fields in front of me look so similar to home that my heart jumps into my throat. "Will I be able to say goodbye to my family?" I ask, but it comes out sounding like a beg.

"No, I'm sorry." Ryne is regretful. "It's too dangerous. If this is going to work, everyone must believe you're dead."

My breath catches, but I still need him to confirm. "You're not going to kill me?"

Ryne growls low. "I could never kill you, Poppy. Never."

"So what now?"

He looks to Knox. Under the moonlight, I can see their features enough to notice an unspoken agreement passing between them.

"Now you run," Ryne says roughly. "You run, and you never look back."

I open and close my mouth, unable to find a response.

"Knox is going with you," he continues. "You won't be alone. He'll make sure you make it to safety."

"Safety? Out there in the wilds? Out with the lycans?" I shake my head. "I can't leave you, Ryne. No. That won't be safe—"

"You are a lycan now," he snaps. "You know this is the only way."

"But—"

"Please don't make it any harder than it has to be."

I'm not trying to make it harder, but there has to be another way. The thought of leaving him and going, running and never looking back, becoming a lycan—it's impossible.

Ryne holds out his hand, and Knox drops the car keys in his palm.

"I'm serious, Poppy," Ryne's voice grows hard. "If you come back to my city, I will kill you myself."

"But you just said you could never kill me," I say.

"I wouldn't have a choice!" His voice booms into the night, rolling across the fields like thunder. This is it. This is the end. How could this be the end?

I don't want to believe it. I can't.

Ryne rushes forward, wraps me into a tight hug, and whispers tenderly against my ear. "I'm sorry. Please be brave for me. Please do this. You can survive out there. You're the strongest woman I know."

I don't feel strong right now. I feel angry, confused, beaten—but not strong. But I have to be, so I nod into his chest, and he lets me go. The weight of that release breaks my heart. I've never felt more alone, even though he still stands a foot away.

And then he's getting in the car, and then he's driving away, and then he's gone.

I turn to Knox. "Are you sure you want to come with me? You can go back. Or you can run away. Whatever you want, I won't judge you."

He stares at me for a long moment, his buzzed blonde hair shining pink under the glow of the blood moon, and he smiles the saddest smile I've ever seen. "I would never do that to you, Poppy."

And then the first boy I ever lost reaches out and takes my hand. His is cold, and mine is burning hot. Together, we turn to face the unknown.

To Be Continued in Rise of the Wild Moon. . .

Dear Reader,

AHHHH! Can you believe it??? What's going to happen to Poppy now? Grab book three, Rise of the Wild Moon here: https://www.amazon.com/dp/B09BBFW79K.

Did you know that Nina and I wrote the first kissing scene in Night of the Wolf Moon in Ryne's point of view as well? If you didn't get a chance to join our groups after book one, this deal is still available. Do you want it? (We know the answer to that question is yes.) To gain access to the file, you'll have to join both of our Facebook groups.

Here is the link for Nina's group: www.facebook.com/ groups/ninasreadingparty and Kim's group: www. facebook.com/groups/KimberlyLothReleaseParty. Happy reading!

If you loved this book, please leave a review and don't forget to tell your friends. Help us spread the word! www.amazon.com/dp/B092W9TG6Q

We weren't quite sure what would happen when we wrote together and we were both surprised to find it was magic. This has been one of our all time favorite books to write.
Love you guys! Thanks for taking this journey with us.

XO,
Kim and Nina

ABOUT THE AUTHOR: NINA WALKER

Nina Walker is a USA Today and Amazon Top 100 Bestselling author. She lives near the beautiful red mountains of southern Utah with her family. She writes across multiple fantasy genres and loves metaphysical magic systems, forbidden love interests, and unexpected plot twists. Nina also co-writes romantic comedy under the pen name, Grace Costello.

Learn more at www.ninawalkerbooks.com & follow her shenanigans on Instagram or TikTok @ninabelievesinmagic.

For early access opportunities and bonus gifts, please join her Facebook reader group "Nina's Reading Party."

ALSO BY KIMBERLY LOTH

The Dragon Kings (Young Adult Paranormal)

The Dragon Kings (original) Series: www.kimberlyloth.com/TDKSeries

The Dragon Kings Boxed Set (all-in-one book): www.kimberlyloth.com/TDKBoxset

The Dragon Kings Boxsets (sequel) Series: **Meet the Next Generation** www.kimberlyloth.com/TDKBoxsetSeries

Circus of the Dead (Young Adult Romantic Thriller)

Circus of the Dead (original) Series: www.kimberlyloth.com/CODSeries

Circus of the Dead Boxed Set (all-in-one book): www.kimberlyloth.com/CODBoxset

Circus of the Dead Boxsets (sequel) Series: **The Show Must Go On** www.kimberlyloth.com/CODBoxsetSeries

The Thorn Chronicles (Young Adult Paranormal)

The Thorn Chronicles Series: www.kimberlyloth.com/TTCSeries

The Thorn Chronicles Boxed Set (all-in-one book): www.kimberlyloth.com/TTCBoxset

Sons of the Sand (Young Adult Paranormal)

Sons of the Sand Series: www.kimberlyloth.com/SOSSeries

Sons of the Sand Boxed Set (all-in-one book): www.kimberlyloth.com/SOSBoxset

Stella and Sol (Young Adult Fantasy)

Stella and Sol Series: www.kimberlyloth.com/SASSeries

Stella and Sol Boxed Set (all-in-one book): www.kimberlyloth.com/SASBoxset

Michigan Millionaires (Sweet Romance Series)

Michigan Millionaires Series: www.kimberlyloth.com/MMSeries

ABOUT THE AUTHOR: KIMBERLY LOTH

Kimberly Loth has lived all over the world. From the isolated woods of the Ozarks to exotic city of Cairo. She currently resides in the beautiful Sugar Creek in southern Missouri, with her husband and her adorable dog Maisy.

She's been writing for twelve years and is the author of the Amazon bestselling series The Dragon Kings. In her free time she volunteers at church, reads, and travels as often as possible.